TIME WILL TELL
A COAST-TO-COAST BRIDES NOVELLA

ANNE MATEER

ZB Zarephath Books

Time Will Tell by Anne Mateer
Published by Zarephath Books
www.zarephathbooks.com

Scripture quotations are from the King James Version of the Bible.

This is a work of fiction.

Cover by Sarah Thompson Designs (photos by Niklas Rhöse and Amador
Loureiro, both on Unsplash)

Ebook ISBN: 978-0-9992322-2-4
Print ISBN: 978-0-9992322-3-1

To all (including myself!) who struggle to trust God with their dreams

He hath made every thing beautiful in his time: also he hath set the world in their heart, so that no man can find out the work that God maketh from the beginning to the end.

— ECCLESIASTES 3:11

CHAPTER 1

Toledo, 1835

"I DON'T WANT to say good-bye," Annis Jackson whispered as she clung to Hugh Hylton in a shadowed corner of a hallway on the steamship *Cleveland*. A porter, laden with trunks and boxes belonging to passengers disembarking in Toledo, clomped down the corridor. Annis hid her face in Hugh's shoulder, not eager to be noticed, even by those who would sail onward to Detroit.

When the echo of boot steps died away, Hugh nudged her chin upward, until she looked full into his face once more.

"It isn't good-bye, darling." A hint of laughter tinged the baritone, which set her stomach tumbling once more.

"But it won't be the same as this." She grabbed his lapels and pressed her forehead into his chest. During her two years at her aunt Delia's Ladies' Seminary in Buffalo, New York, she and Mr. Hylton had crossed paths several times, always with a pull of attraction. But meeting like this—on the ship, with Annis's chaperone confined to their room with seasickness—had afforded them three glorious, unfettered days in one another's company as they'd crossed Lake Erie, deepening their acquaintance, confirming their mutual feelings.

She searched his eyes once more, noting every fleck of gold brightening the rich brown, and groaned. "It will be so hard knowing you are nearby yet still beyond reach."

"Beyond reach? I'll be nearer than ever before!" His arms circled her waist and drew her closer still. She felt his heartbeat beneath her cheek, his whisper near her ear. "I'll approach your father the moment we disembark and secure his permission to court you."

Annis sucked in a sharp breath and pushed away, both palms flat on his chest. "Please, Hugh. Please let me . . . prepare him. You don't know how—" she swallowed hard "—how much he despises your uncle." She shook her head, tears clogging her throat and stinging her eyes as Hugh's expression reflected his confusion.

She ought to have told him the minute he mentioned his relation to Mr. Benjamin Franklin Stickney, but she'd been unwilling to mar their idyllic days. Now how could she find the words to explain the antagonism between her father and Hugh's uncle?

Clinging to him, she grappled for words to buy her time. "I-I fear Pa will forbid us to marry before he even has a chance to know you, just because of your relation to that man."

"Surely you exaggerate, dearest." He planted a kiss on the top of her head. "Whatever the disagreement between my uncle and your father, it has nothing to do with us."

Annis bit her lip. If Hugh didn't understand, this could go badly. Very, very badly.

Hugh pulled her close. "And if you mean their political leanings, don't worry, Annis. You already informed me that your father staunchly opposes Ohio's claim to Toledo, which my uncle supports. Is that the only issue?"

Annis stiffened. How could he understand the rancor between her father and his uncle? How could anyone who hadn't lived in the narrow triangle of land between the state of Ohio and the territory of Michigan? Bitterness infected both sides of the Michigan-Ohio debate. The people of Toledo—most of them anyway—had strong feelings about who ought to have jurisdiction over their strip of land, with its access to Lake Erie and planned canals.

"It's just a line on a map, Annis." He spoke softly, as if she were a skittish colt or a small child. His hand cupped her elbow and eased her toward him again. "A line fought over by men with little else to do, I fear."

But Annis knew that "line" he spoke of so glibly divided more than just land. It divided hearts.

If only her father and his uncle, the two who were once such close friends, weren't so firmly entrenched in opposite loyalties.

"Please, Hugh. Please trust me. Let me prepare Pa. Let me ease him into an understanding of us. Please?"

He pulled back, traced the curve of her jaw with his thumb as she watched the battle raging behind his eyes. He was a stickler for truth, one of the reasons he'd been drawn to the newspaper business. And thanks to his uncle's generosity, he'd be in charge of his own paper, *The Toledo Herald*. There would be no hiding his identity—or his politics—from Pa.

But what if she could sway the skirmish between her father and his uncle? After all, they were both reasonable men in every other regard. If she—and Hugh—could foster an understanding between the two men, an agreement to abide amicably even while in disagreement, perhaps they could end the animosity within Toledo as well. Encourage the people of Toledo to live peaceably together, no matter where the men in Washington decided to draw the state line.

Yes, it was a good plan. A *godly* plan, one promoting unity and brotherhood. Annis's tumult of emotion settled as determination took root. Pa always said her tenacity of spirit when she found something she wanted would make Old Hickory himself seem malleable. She could do this. *They* could do this. She opened her mouth to spout her optimism, then closed it and shuddered.

What if Pa discovered her attachment to Hugh before the reconciliation succeeded? She feared more than his disapproval. She feared his disappointment. His questioning of her loyalty to their family. To him.

Just as she stiffened with fear, the tight line of Hugh's mouth softened. "How long do you anticipate it will take to prepare him? If it requires much time, I fear I'll lose patience and seek him out myself, for I don't want to live a day beyond what I must without you."

The thrill of being loved gave way quickly to a hard frown. Preparing Pa was only half the battle. She'd have to enlist Hugh's help with his uncle, too. They would need to foster a mutual coming together of their relations. And that could take time.

The steamship whistle shrilled. Annis pressed a quick kiss to his mouth. "I have to go. Mrs. Williamson will be looking for me. But don't worry. I'll come to you soon. Even if I have to sneak out of the house under cover of night."

Hugh grabbed her hand just before she stepped beyond reach. "Take care, Annis. Don't allow any rash action to hinder our future together."

Even as she nodded, Annis knew her response didn't truly reflect her heart. For no matter the risk, she would pursue every possible opportunity to spend time with the man who'd stolen her heart.

∿

"ANNIS, DEAR!" Ma's voice carrying on the cold air birthed tears as Annis ran down the gangplank and into her waiting arms. Oh, how she'd missed her mother! She pressed her face into the elegant lace collar, savoring the scent of rose and lavender.

Behind her, Pa's deep voice thanked Mrs. Williamson for her

care of his daughter. Annis smirked into her mother's shoulder. If he only knew.

Then the familiar timbre drew nearer. "Come, Gwendolyn. I'm sure it's my turn to greet our girl."

As Annis turned, she spied the twinkle in her father's eye, the twitch of a grin on his lips. He swooped in, lifted her from the ground and swung her in a circle before setting her down again.

"I knew you'd be the toast of the seminary." His breath puffed white in the air as his chest expanded like a rooster's. "Your aunt Delia said she had nothing left to teach you so you might as well come home. Which is fine with me, for I have plenty to keep you occupied. Who knows? After working with me, perhaps you'll be the first female attorney in the new state of Michigan." His laughter bellowed into the noisy wharf, drawing sideways glances from other passengers and their welcoming parties.

Annis hid a nervous giggle behind her hand. Pa did make a stir wherever he went, whether it be waxing eloquent on the value of women's education or the up-and-coming fortunes of the territory—soon, hopefully, to be the state—of Michigan. And she had no doubt he firmly believed every word he said.

Suddenly she imagined introducing Hugh to Pa, and her gaze dropped to the ground. It would cause an unmitigated row. Pa's raised voice. Ma's tears. And Philippa—would her younger sister chastise or co-conspire?

Before she could settle on an answer to that question, a squeal rent the air just before a body flung itself at her, nearly knocking her off her feet.

"Oh, Annis! I'm so, so glad you're home! You can't know how I've missed you!" Philippa squealed again, her arms tightening around Annis's neck, cutting off her breath. Then her sister let go as quickly as she had attached herself. Grabbing Annis's hand, Philippa pulled her ahead of their parents, words flying from her mouth at such a pace that Annis couldn't sort them into any coherent order.

"Whoa, Philly." Annis yanked on her sister's hand. Philippa came stumbling back to where Annis stood firm.

Philippa grinned, then sighed. "I've missed our old joke. You're the only one who calls me Philly, you know."

"I know." Annis's smile widened. "We have one whole summer together before *you* go off to Aunt Delia's school. And I intend to tease you every single day before you board that ship. Otherwise, you might imagine yourself destined for easy success."

Philippa's laughter—no ladylike giggle for her—rang out clear. Then she looped her arm around Annis's and strode toward their home at the edge of town, her steps as long as skirts and petticoats and corsets would allow. Annis almost ran to keep up, even as she twisted around, seeking one last glance of Hugh.

There—just at the bottom of the gangplank, shaking hands with fellow passengers also taking leave of the steamship. Their eyes met. They shared a smile. Then Philippa tugged her forward again, leaving Annis no choice but to pay attention to the direction of her feet.

"You must tell me all about Buffalo and Aunt Delia's school. I mean everything you didn't already write in your letters. I know you went to some house dances and dinner parties, but you didn't mention the men you met, for I'm sure you met men. Weren't any of them dashingly handsome or delightfully clever enough to attract your attention? And don't tell me you were just in Buffalo to study!" Philippa rolled her eyes.

Annis giggled and pressed closer to her sister, the way they'd always done when there was a confidence to be shared. The desire to reveal her secret love nearly loosened her tongue, but she captured her bottom lip with her teeth before the words escaped.

Philippa wasn't the best secret-keeper in town, but she was as loyal as a spaniel. And Annis and Hugh would need allies.

"Of course there were men, Philly." Annis fiddled with the folds of her skirt to avoid her sister's eager eyes.

"And?" Philippa practically bounced as she walked. "You can't stop there, Annis. It's simply—well, it's simply cruel."

Annis sucked in a deep breath and glanced behind them. Ma and Pa followed, but slowly. Sedately. Giving Annis and Philippa plenty of room for a private conversation.

She didn't want to outright lie. Maybe she could tell the truth without the details. Her mind whirled with ideas, finally settling on: "Buffalo has the most handsome, most intelligent men I've ever met."

Philippa snorted. "Not hard if you've only ever been here."

Annis wrinkled her nose at her sister as the familiar gable of their home broke into view. She glanced at Philippa, spied the competition in her sister's eyes, and broke into a run toward the porch. But Philippa charged close behind, edging ahead, her hand slapping the top step a hairsbreadth before Annis's.

"First!" Philippa shouted, per the rules of their childhood game.

"Gently, girls!" Ma's cultured admonition carried on the frigid breeze.

Annis's gaze met her sister's, and they dissolved into peals of laughter.

CHAPTER 2

EACH CREAK of the pulley rope holding the heavy crate above the wharf wrenched Hugh's heart and tightened his muscles. Slowly, the large wooden box lowered toward the dock, men shifting around it, guiding it. Hugh's jaw clenched.

Almost.

There.

The thud of the cargo hitting the surface echoed across the din.

"Have a care!" Hugh shouted into the icy wind sluicing across the water. Only after a beefy arm rose and waved in his direction could Hugh force himself to move. "It's only my livelihood, lads," he mumbled as he rubbed the back of his neck, suddenly warm in spite of the March morning chill. His new Albion iron hand press might not have had the softest of landings, but at least it was here. As was Hugh.

And Annis.

He smiled, picturing again the effusive greeting her family had given her as he'd watched from the hatch atop the gangway. He'd wanted so badly to inch closer, force Annis to acknowledge and introduce him.

But he hadn't. And she didn't.

Anyway, he'd agreed to give her time. And Hugh always kept his word.

His hand strayed to the pocket of his overcoat, fingering again the unexpected letter from his uncle. *We are in need of a newspaper in this town. With my money and your expertise, I think we can make a go of it.*

Hugh's chest expanded. Editor of his own newspaper. At the ripe old age of four and twenty. A turn of events he hadn't imagined possible, but one that would allow him to plan for the future—a future he now couldn't imagine without Annis.

No matter that he'd not yet met his mother's brother. They were kin, and apparently that was enough. That and the reputation Hugh had acquired working for the Buffalo paper. Uncle Stickney's confidence bolstered Hugh's belief that he could make a name for himself. For his newspaper. But would his professional success be enough to win over Annis's father, secure his blessing to make her his wife?

He wasn't sure. Couldn't be until he'd actually met the man. But after watching his reunion with his daughter, Hugh felt sure Mr. Jackson would desire Annis's happiness.

Hope turned his steps jaunty as he searched the dock for a face that put him in mind of his mother. No visage stirred familiarity, but that didn't mean his uncle wasn't here. Hugh wandered through the crowd, met the gaze of several men. Nodded. Tipped his hat. No one approached in recognition. Or even in question. No one person appeared to mill about as if in search of an unknown.

Hugh's fortitude flagged. Had he given his uncle the wrong time? The wrong date? But surely he would seek out the ship's schedule to confirm. Why, then, wouldn't his uncle be here to greet him?

Hugh shivered with a blast of cold air. Perhaps his uncle expected a man such as Hugh to make his own way forward, believing his uncle would find him eventually. Yes, that had to be the case. Therefore, he ought to proceed directly to the storefront that had been prepared for his arrival. His uncle might even be there overseeing the final details.

After speaking with the freight man and securing delivery of both his press and his trunk, Hugh started through the streets of the town he would now call home, his enthusiasm waning with every step. Toledo was a newer town than Buffalo, but he'd not expected anything quite so . . . unrefined. Oh, there were buildings laid out in rows on a grid of streets, but streets covered only in earth. Buildings crafted mostly of unpainted boards. Piles of refuse whose stench wafted on each gust of breeze.

Still, every town had to start somewhere. Like a baby who grows into a boy, then a man. These dwellings and thoroughfares would soon reflect a new maturity. As would the citizenry. They'd abandon this childish quarrel over territorial rights and function as a community. And Hugh would be a part of that maturing process, using his newspaper to foster understanding.

But first he had to persuade them he had news worth reading.

FIFTEEN MINUTES LATER, Hugh stood in the dusty street, his heart sinking to his knees. From the brief correspondence with his uncle, Hugh hadn't thought him a man who would throw a building together haphazardly. But the evidence stood in front of him. Rough wood siding rising two stories above ground, without even a coat of whitewash. Gaps between boards not nailed on a straight line. At least there was real glass in the window, though the painted letters arched across it weren't of uniform size or spacing.

How would anyone take him seriously in a place like this? His insides turned as cold as his extremities, almost freezing him in place. He didn't move until the delivery wagon pulled to a stop in front of him, blocking his view of the ramshackle building. His eyes rested on the crated printing press, reminding him that this was the most significant part of his uncle's investment in this venture. And Hugh intended to make it earn its keep. Not only because he needed a nest egg with which to support Annis, but because he would now also need the capital to make his place of business respectable.

He'd even settle for presentable.

Hugh let out a deep breath, leaving his shoulders in a slump. At least he'd requested living quarters connected to the office, so he knew there would be a roof over his head. Something to be thankful for.

Fishing the key from his pocket, the one delivered to him two weeks ago by his cousin, Two Stickney, who had been passing through Buffalo on business, Hugh shook his head, wondering again what made his uncle name his sons One and Two. In spite of years of his mother's needling and cajoling, her brother had never given any adequate explanation.

The door opened with a groan that mimicked Hugh's. Nothing inside had been cleaned up after the hasty construction. He stepped over discarded boards, bent nails, and piles of sawdust. After an assessment of the main room, he made his way out the back of the building to find a small, bricked kitchen building and a flight of stairs leading to living quarters above the office.

After a quick inspection of the kitchen walls, Hugh was more impressed with the masonry than he'd been with the siding on the building. Then he climbed the stairs and entered a large room nestled beneath the gabled roof.

"We'll see when it rains," Hugh mumbled, descending after one of the freight men called his name.

He met them in the front room, six men layered with dirt and sweat. After a lengthy discussion they decided to uncrate the large iron press and disassemble it, then bring it inside piece by piece to reconstruct. Hugh showed the men where to place it before they trudged back out to begin their task.

Using a discarded scrap of lumber as a makeshift broom, Hugh cleared the floor along the back wall. Then, as the press slowly took shape, he surveyed the square room, pictured it laid out as a real newspaper office.

With his boot, he drew a line in the dirt on the floor, situated about a quarter of the way into the room. There he'd build a long counter to separate the press from the public. Behind would be plenty of space for the work of typesetting and printing, for storing paper and boxes of type. Room for a desk and a chair.

He grinned. Two chairs. For once he and Annis were married, she desired to help. And he believed she could. He'd heard of her work at the Buffalo Ladies' Seminary and surmised her to be at least as good of a writer as himself. Maybe better.

Hugh rubbed the back of his neck. If his dream of working alongside Annis as his wife had any chance of coming true, he'd better get started. Perhaps he ought to begin at the mercantile down the street. They'd have most of what he needed. And perhaps even know of a young man eager to work hard and learn the printing trade.

After paying the freight men, locking up the building, and pocketing the key, Hugh started down the street with more optimistic eyes. Toledo was already populated with a variety of businesses. Mercantile. Harness shop. Barber shop. Even a hotel. A bookshop and Mr. Jackson's law practice attested to the fact that there would, indeed, be some members of Toledo society who had at least a brush with culture and education—beyond his uncle and cousins.

As he turned into the mercantile, he noticed again the row of warehouses near the water's edge attesting to the anticipation of the canal connecting the Maumee River to Lake Erie. Toledo was well-placed for an economic boom, and Hugh's newspaper would be poised to chronicle it all.

Yes, Toledo would be his paradise. His and Annis's.

If only Annis's concern over the contention between her father and his uncle didn't stir such disquiet within him.

CHAPTER 3

ANNIS PRESSED her fingertips and nose against the window glass in her father's office, her gaze roaming what she could see of St. Clair Street. A few pedestrians. A few wagons or other conveyances.

No Hugh.

Though she knew he was busy setting up shop and that, in that last moment before they'd parted on the ship, they'd agreed to keep their distance until she had prepared her father, she'd imagined catching a glimpse of him now and then. She'd pictured Hugh dashing after news stories, making trips to the mercantile to outfit his office. But after a week without a glimpse of her beloved, Annis wasn't sure she could adhere any longer to their agreed-upon separation. Especially since she hadn't yet fully enlisted his help in her plan. Or figured out a way to approach Pa with the news.

Groaning, she rested her forehead against the glass, let her breath cloud the street scene.

"Annis Jackson! What are you doing to my clean window?"

Annis spun to face her father, fingers locked behind her back, bottom lip caught between her teeth. She felt ten years old again, being scolded for forgetting to wipe the mud from her shoes before entering the house. Pa had less tolerance for a mess than Ma did.

"Sorry, Pa. I'll clean it. I promise." She glanced back, lifted her arm and used her sleeve to rub the mass of smudges. Marring Pa's picture window wasn't the way to soften his heart.

She flashed him a tight smile and returned to the desk he'd set up for her. Doing her work well would boost her esteem in Pa's eyes. Especially if she could, indeed, take the place of his elderly scrivener, whose work tended, now, to unsightly corrections. Pa liked a clean copy of a legal document written in a neat hand, much as he liked an unsullied view through his window.

Glancing outside again, she wondered what errand might take her down Huron Street, past the building Hugh's uncle had secured for the new paper. Surely Pa had a message to deliver somewhere in town. Annis turned to her father, determined to find an excuse to leave the office alone, but his look stopped her words.

Head cocked, eyes narrowed, he seemed to be trying to peer into her head and see her thoughts. "You haven't been quite yourself since arriving home, Annis. Is something troubling you?"

Heat flooding her face, she shuffled through a stack of papers on the desk. "Of course not, Pa. I'm just getting used to being home again." She sat down, opened the copybook, and smoothed a page to begin transcription of the next letter, hoping he hadn't spied the rosiness in her cheeks that usually accompanied her lies. She waited until the warmth receded before raising her face again. "I'm fine. I promise."

But guilt niggled in her chest. While she wanted to ease her father into her secret, that also meant keeping the news from her mother. And she hated keeping secrets from Ma. Especially this secret. For while Ma had agreed with Pa's desire that his daughter receive an education, she hadn't wavered in her open desire for them to find husbands, either. Good, strong, intelligent, faith-filled men who would walk through the ups and downs of life with them.

Annis smiled at her father. He nodded but didn't look entirely convinced she was telling the truth. Then he sighed. "I suspect you miss your friends. And your studies."

A bit of Annis's tension dissipated. She could respond with some honesty. After all, Hugh was her friend, and she missed talking with him. Lacing together her fingers, she settled her gaze on her father and hoped her expression conveyed reassurance. "I do. Terribly. I am so grateful you sent me to Aunt Delia's school. You know that, don't you?"

"Yes, dear child." He stepped closer, cupped Annis's chin. "I just want you to be happy. That's all."

"I am happy, Pa. So happy to be home with you all." She stood, kissed his cheek then pulled away, blinking back stubborn tears and clearing the huskiness from her throat before pasting on a bright smile. "Now if you'll excuse me, I believe I have quite a task ahead of me to get these letters penned into the copybook so they can be sent."

Before he could reply—or continue to pry—Annis returned to her seat, dipped a pen in the inkwell, and began to write.

∾

Two hours later, Philippa strolled into the office, a basket swinging on her arm.

"I thought you needed a shopping break." She held the basket aloft, the mischievous sparkle in her smile igniting Annis's desire to leave work to be with her sister. Sixteen seemed so much more carefree than twenty.

Taking a quiet step, then two, she peeked into Pa's office. Head bent toward the desk, Pa frantically scratched words across a piece of paper, stopping only for a new dip in the ink.

Turning back to her sister, she whispered, "I don't think I should leave."

"Oh, pish!" Philippa flounced past her, into the office, her voice carrying back to Annis. "Pa, I've come for Annis. I need her to help me pick out—"

Annis arrived at the door in time to see her father wave his hand without raising his head.

"Thank you, Pa." Philippa pressed a kiss to his head and returned to Annis with a smug smile. "See? All taken care of. Now grab your mantle and let's go."

Annis quickly marked her place and arranged the papers so she could resume her task in the morning. Then she shrugged into her cloak and hurried down the board walkway after her sister.

~

THEY STOPPED at the milliner's to order new hats, at the mercantile to arrange delivery of a few groceries for Ma, at the bookstore to procure a new novel. By the time Philippa allowed Annis a say in their activity, the milky afternoon sun had given way to more clouds. And a deeper chill.

"I'm awfully cold, Annis. Let's head home."

Annis hummed agreement but kept moving forward. She'd managed to steer them onto Huron Street toward Swan Creek. They passed over Monroe Street, Pa's office just two blocks behind them now. Phillippa protested again. This time Annis held the shopping basket as Philippa wrapped her scarf more tightly around her neck. Then Annis continued toward Washington Street, Philippa's objections barely registering. Only one more block until Toledo turned into unbroken creek bank.

"Annis!" Philippa stamped her foot on the board walkway. "Where are you going? There is nothing—"

Annis grabbed Philippa's hand and yanked her forward. A

few more steps, and then she found *Toledo Herald* stenciled on glass.

"Whoa, Philly!" Annis brought them to a stop directly across the wide, earthen street from the sloppily lettered window. Annis frowned. Pa would hate the lack of attention to detail on the sign. As would Hugh. And he likely wasn't happy over the shoddy appearance of the structure, either.

"Annis, what—"

"Hush, Philly." Pushing up on her toes, Annis squinted, trying to peer through the window. Was he in there? From this distance, she couldn't discern anything but shadow.

Philippa tugged at Annis's arm. "What are you looking at?"

Tight-lipped, Annis glanced at her sister. She'd mentioned her friend from the steamship a couple of times over the past few days, but hadn't elaborated. Maybe it was time . . .

Annis pulled Philippa's arm, dragging her toward Lafayette Street. "We'll go a little farther this way. I want to see how things have changed. Please?"

Philippa shrugged, eyes rolling toward the sky. "Whatever you say. But there's nothing in this poky town that compares to Buffalo. Especially all the way out here."

Annis grinned and strode onward, Philippa following along dutifully. They reached the end of the street. The burgeoning grasses and trees leading to the banks of Swan Creek gave off a subtle smell of springtime, of coming growth. As Annis took in the scent, she wondered if it actually existed or was only a reflection of the nearness of Hugh.

Philippa turned Annis back the way they'd come, but Annis wasn't giving up yet. "Let's cross to the other side for the journey home."

"Why? There isn't anything over there, not even a walkway. Just dirt that will require me to brush my skirt before I wear it again." Philippa shook out said skirt, preening a bit before glancing around to see if there was anyone to notice.

"I'll brush your skirt and mine." Annis pulled her pouting

sister across the street. A little work was a small price to pay for a possible glimpse of Hugh. Philippa trudged the dirty path, mumbling under her breath and tugging the brim of her hat a bit lower.

As they neared the newspaper office, Annis turned her head in its direction. "Oh, look. A newspaper and printing office. How wonderful!"

Philippa snorted. "Not to hear Pa tell of it."

Annis's attention snapped back to her sister, her heart pounding in fearful anticipation. The obvious question almost choked her as it climbed from her throat. "What do you mean?"

Philippa glanced around before leaning close to Annis's ear. "It's one of *their* papers. You know. Ohioan. At least that's the word around town. I heard some derelict relative of nasty Mr. Stickney is to be in charge of that rag. Pa is fit to be tied, but what can he do?"

"Do?" Annis heard the higher timbre of her own voice, unease crawling closer to the surface. Derelict relative? Nasty Mr. Stickney? That rag?

Oh, dear. Oh, dear.

Annis swallowed hard and tried to nudge her sister toward the way of reason. "Why should he *do* anything? The territory of Michigan resides under the jurisdiction of the United States of America, where even those we disagree with have a right to say what they think."

Philippa shrugged and began walking, not seeming to notice Annis's dismay—or her stumble to follow.

This was exactly what Annis had feared. She would definitely need time to soften Pa to Hugh. And reconciliation with Mr. Stickney would be key.

She must speak with Hugh. Soon. For if he felt as bereft of her presence as she did of his, he might come looking for her and run into Pa instead.

If only the news of the *Herald's* backing had remained a secret until after Pa had a chance to meet Hugh, deem him an intelligent and reasonable man in spite of an uncle who disagreed—albeit vehemently—with Pa over the fate of a fairly small strip of land that butted up against Lake Erie.

But apparently that ship had already sailed.

Annis sighed. It was more important than ever that she keep Hugh from her father. Otherwise, she'd end up a broken-hearted, blue-stocking spinster working as Pa's scrivener for the rest of her life—in the state of Michigan, if Pa had his way.

"Let's go back," Annis blurted. "I—I've always wanted to see a printing press at work."

Philippa started to protest, but Annis whirled around and returned to the clumsily painted window. She pressed her face to the glass, cupping her hands around her eyes to block the glare. A counter bisected the room, the wood shavings on the floor nearby testifying to its newness. A large iron press loomed along the back wall. A broom stood in one corner.

But no Hugh.

Philippa tugged at Annis's sleeve. "Let's go home. I'm shivering."

Annis sighed as she backed away from the glass. If she couldn't see Hugh, she could at least write to him. Establish an opportunity for them to meet, to talk. For now, that plan would have to do.

CHAPTER 4

HUGH SURVEYED the results of a week—minus the Sabbath—of backbreaking, sweaty work. The newspaper office was ready for business. A counter now separated customer space from working space, a half-gate at one end allowing him access from the front to the back of the room. The printing press gleamed with newness while the smell of sawn wood hung in the air, though the floors had been swept clean of debris. And not a single smudge marked the plate glass window. The crooked letters still rankled, but he could fix that—as soon as the paper turned a profit.

The large table near the press would serve as Hugh's desk. Drawers of typeface lined the opposite wall. The newly hired man, Sid, would arrange those letters to match Hugh's written words, then together they would ink the plates, crank the paper through, hang the sheets to dry.

A newspaper would be born.

His newspaper.

Hugh waited for the chest-swelling triumph he'd expected to feel, but it didn't come. In truth, he could think of nothing but Annis at the moment.

She'd sent a note by the hand of a small boy the evening before last. He'd smiled at the scribbled news of her job in her father's office—news nestled among more personal endearments —then redoubled his efforts to prepare for the first edition. For he'd vowed not to reply to Annis until he could open the doors of his place of business and inspire her confidence in him.

In them.

He looked around once more, satisfied he had achieved his goal in that regard.

Sid, a jovial twenty-year-old with plenty of brawn and enough brains to suffice, entered through the back door, his arms weighted down by cotton paper. With a grunt, he lowered himself closer to the floor before dropping the load with a thud atop the oilcloth spread across the wood planks. Then he stood, stretched his arms to the ceiling and arched his back before running a hand over the iron arm of the press.

"Now all you have to do is find some news." Sid's jaunty grin twisted Hugh's belly into a tight knot. It would, indeed, take more than an office to make a newspaper. So he best get started.

"Right you are, Sid." Hugh slid a notebook from the corner of his desk and chose a pencil from the box on the shelf beneath the counter. "Wish me luck!"

Sid pulled a stool closer to the counter and sat. "Just think of me twiddling my thumbs—and getting paid for it."

Hugh's eyebrows lifted. "That will, indeed, be a motivation. I know only too well what trouble can find an un-industrious young man." Hugh had found his own share of trouble—until he'd discovered his calling in collecting and sharing the news. Maybe the same would happen for Sid. He seemed to be a nice kid, willing to work hard and learn. Together, they could make the *Herald* into a paper to be proud of.

And that thought led his mind back to Annis. Hugh examined his pencil to hide a frown. At the end of her note, she'd begged to meet, to talk, but he couldn't allow her to come here, not with Sid around. Not if they wanted to keep their relationship secret, as she'd also emphasized.

Staring at the ceiling through most of every night since they'd landed, wishing he could see Annis, hold her in his arms, had almost convinced him to disregard her desire for concealment. And yet, he also realized it wouldn't be a bad thing to establish the paper and his reputation before he met her father.

His collar suddenly felt tight around his neck. A newspaper needed more than a printed edition. It needed subscribers—or at least consistent customers—to prosper. Could he garner such loyalty from the citizens of Toledo? Would he immediately lose the patronage of everyone who disagreed with his uncle's stance on the Ohio-Michigan debate? He'd have to win over the Michiganders for the paper to thrive. And Annis—and her father—could help him do that.

He turned to Sid once more. "You have the price sheet should anyone inquire about printing? Name cards and the like?"

Sid nodded, patted the sheet on the counter in front of him. "I'm all set. Go on, now. Rustle us up something to do. Advertisements, if you can't find actual news worth writing." The boy puckered his lips and began to whistle as he clasped his hands and his thumbs circled one another.

Hugh smiled. Sid had the natural bent of a man of business, already looking toward a source of revenue, not just to news. Hugh turned to the door, anxious to begin his search for information worthy enough to justify space in ink. Maybe he'd even catch a glimpse of Annis on the street, perhaps hear her voice. The thought filled him with joy. With desire. But before he could embark on his quest, the office's front door swung open, the bell he'd hung above jingling in announcement.

"Well, this looks splendid." A man dressed in a finely tailored suit with an incongruously scruffy beard and weathered face stepped inside, a gold watch chain trailing across his elaborate waistcoat. He looked about him with an air of . . . ownership.

Uncle Stickney? Hugh swallowed hard. He'd given up on the man's courtesy—and involvement. Made all the choices himself. Perhaps too quickly.

The man strutted up and down in front of the counter, offering no other greeting, no introduction. Perhaps this wasn't his uncle after all.

As the man scrutinized the room, his hands clutched his lapels, and he rocked back on his heels. "Mighty fine job you've done here." He spun to meet Hugh's gaze. "When will we see the first issue in hand?"

Heat crawled up Hugh's neck, over his chin, cheeks, ears. All the way to his hairline. Ought he greet the man who hadn't greeted him? Or continue on, greetings aside? He cleared his throat, unable to bid himself to do business without courtesy.

"Good day, sir." He extended his hand, but the man ignored the gesture. "I very much appreciate your interest in our endeavor. May I introduce myself? Hugh Hylton, editor."

The man nodded once, his astute gaze boring into Hugh's until Hugh squirmed.

"Yes. Well." Hugh cleared his throat. "As to the first issue, I was on my way to search out advertisers and news. Until I find those, I can't give a certain date, but I hope it will not be a week hence."

Indeed, he hoped it would be much sooner.

With a quick spin, the man put his attention on Sid. "And you'll be running the operations?"

Sid's Adam's apple bobbed in his thin neck as his gaze cut to Hugh's. "Learning to, sir. I mean to help with the typesetting. A-And the printing."

"Always good to have an apprentice willing to learn." The man pinned Hugh with his gaze again. "I trust you know what you are doing?"

Hugh's mouth dropped open, but he had no idea how to

answer. *Yes* seemed a bit overconfident. *No*, well, he got the distinct impression this man—his uncle?—wouldn't favor that as an answer, either.

Suddenly their visitor threw back his head and laughed. "You'll do, boy. You'll do. Enough of my sister's *niceness* in you to appeal to the rabble in this town." He clapped Hugh on the shoulder, nodded to Sid, and was gone, leaving Hugh and Sid staring at each another in bewilderment.

"I guess that was my uncle. And I suppose that means he approves." Hugh scratched his head, wondering if his enigmatic uncle would return anytime soon or want further input on the running of the newspaper. Then he shrugged. Whether Uncle Stickney appeared in the office often or never didn't matter. He had entrusted Hugh to make a success of the paper.

Sid's whistling started up once more, prompting Hugh to slip out the door onto the primitive street. He intended to make both his uncle and Annis proud. That meant digging into work. But not until he made at least one attempt to see Annis.

CHAPTER 5

ANNIS TRIED to keep her mind on the words she transcribed into the copybook, but they were just letters strung together, separated by spaces. Her fingers itched to close around the inkwell, fling it across the room. Her feet longed to flee into the streets of Toledo in search of her heart's desire. How could Pa have thought this a worthy occupation after the education he'd so tenaciously sought for her? Anyone with a decent hand and keen eye could copy. She needed more. She needed activity for her mind.

She set aside her pen and rubbed her eyes.

Was Hugh as miserable without her as she was without him?

She pulled her gaze to her father's office door. The only way out of this misery was to talk with him, introduce the topic of men in general, Hugh specifically. But the thought struck her dumb with fear. She didn't want to lose Hugh, but she didn't want to alienate her family, either. She wanted them both.

Maybe she ought to begin with understanding the enmity between Pa and Mr. Stickney. She vaguely remembered their friendship, had heard whispered speculation on the reasons for its dissolution. But she didn't know the whole story. Not from the source. Hugh had told her that was key in his business—getting news from a direct source.

Best to start here and now if she hoped to help Hugh with the paper when they were married. She nodded once, as if to persuade herself of her rightness then quickly finished copying the final sentence of the current letter in front of her. Nothing would soften Pa's heart like completed work.

Leaving the copy book open on her desk, she picked up the original letter and crossed the room, then knocked on the half-closed door of her father's private office space.

"Pa?" She stepped into the room before he could answer. He sat hunched over his massive desk, scribbling, one finger in the air to let her know he needed to finish his thought. She counted the beats of her heart until he leaned back in his chair, his face lighting with a wide smile.

"Daughter. What a delightful sight."

Guilt drew Annis's gaze to her feet. She spied the paper in her hand, stepped to the desk and held it out to him.

"Finished already? I must say, you are an improvement over Mr. Jenkins." He shook his head. "It would have taken him hours to complete this contract." His attention returned to the document in front of him, but Annis remained where she stood.

"Yes?" Pa's scruffy eyebrows scrunched closer together. "Is there something more? I thought you had a stack—"

"Oh, I do, Pa." Annis clasped her hands together near her waist. If she didn't broach the subject now, she feared she never would. She took a deep breath, pushed the words past the knot of anxiety in her chest. "But I was wondering if you'd explain to me more of the Ohio-Michigan debate."

Annis startled as the words landed in her own ears. Not quite the way she'd meant to bring up the subject of Hugh, but getting closer. From here, she ought to be able to steer the conversation toward Mr. Stickney. But she'd have to do it quickly, or Pa would lose patience with the interruption.

He set his pen on the blotter and rubbed his eyes. "I informed you of the rudimentary issues in my letters, did I not? What more do you need to know?"

"I—well—" Annis swallowed hard. He'd given her the opportunity to ask her question without preamble. She lifted her chin a tad, posturing the confidence she didn't quite feel. "I wanted to know why you and Mr. Stickney remain such virulent enemies. We all live in Toledo. We all want what is best for our town. Why can we not come together over that and leave the legalities to the men in Washington to sort out?"

Pa pointed to the wooden chair angled in front of his desk. She sat, every part of her body motionless. Every part except her right heel, which bounced with fevered anticipation of his answer.

"I suppose you were too young to understand, and now that you are grown, I forgot you didn't know." Clasped hands on his desk, he leaned forward, as she'd watched him do with clients on numerous occasions. "Mr. Stickney and I once agreed on the growth and flourishing of Toledo. In fact, he used his silver-tipped tongue to persuade us as new settlers on the rim of Lake Erie to throw in our lot with the up-and-coming territory of Michigan, to work for her rightful claim to this strip of land. Until Michigan didn't suit his purposes any longer. Then he switched his allegiance to Ohio."

Pa's intense gaze pinned Annis to her seat like an insect to a specimen board, stopping even her foot from bobbing. Breath trapped in her chest, Annis couldn't even find the strength to blink.

Then Pa's rigidity melted in front of her eyes. He slumped in his chair, brought a hand to his forehead, as if pushing back pain. "It was his duplicity that wrecked our friendship, not his politics. I had assumed him a man of honor, like myself. One whose word once given was kept, not matter the consequence. I had built up a business among those in Michigan territory. To dissolve my association with them then would have meant our financial ruin. So I didn't follow his lead to embrace Ohio's claim to our land. And he couldn't forgive me for that. Whether it was the thwarting of his imagined authority or that he had already promised our support to those in Ohio, I know not. And care not. It was enough of a fissure to cause a complete break between us, a moving apart on both sides."

Annis brightened, her spine snapping straight and tall. "Then—then you don't hate him?"

"I didn't say that," Pa growled. "The man has no allegiance, no determination to see through a course of action he's decided upon. And that I cannot abide in any man, especially one I call my friend." He slapped his palm to his desk, the loud report jarring Annis from her seat. He stood as well and paced the small room, hands deep in the pockets of his trousers. "Now he's funded a newspaper that will not only distribute his poison to everyone in the vicinity but will provide him financial gain in the process."

He spun and faced her, a glint in his eye that sent a jolt of fear from her head to her toes. "But don't you worry." He pointed his long finger at her, as if she were the enemy instead of Mr. Stickney. "I've sent word to Governor Stevens."

Annis bit her trembling lip. Why did Michigan's governor need to know about a newspaper in Toledo, even if it was funded by a staunch Ohioan? Was this really about two men's ideological disagreements? Or was there something more? Even as she held her own father in high esteem, she realized that he, too, had something at stake. He had connections in power in Michigan territory that would be lost to him as a citizen of Ohio. Just as Mr. Stickney fought to protect the opposite for himself.

The thought unsettled her all the more as she considered her own situation. If Pa viewed Mr. Stickney's support of Ohio as a betrayal of their friendship, what would he think of Annis's choice of Hugh?

With a mumbled excuse about finishing her work, Annis skittered to her desk, eager to think through all the implications of what she'd just learned. Pulling a document from the drawer and turning to a fresh page of the copybook, Annis thanked God that her work didn't require her complete concentration.

CHAPTER 6

IF HUGH HAD EVER WANTED to curse, it was now. He'd walked
the entire town, introduced himself to business owners and their
customers, touted the need for an up-and-coming town like
Toledo to boast a newspaper of its own, but the first question
out of everyone's mouth had nothing to do with the paper at all.
It had to do with that infernal line on a map.

"You for Ohio or Michigan?" The first storekeeper he'd
approached had eyed him suspiciously, the few midday
customers ceasing their activity and conversation and fixing
their attention on Hugh.

"Does it matter?" Hugh responded.

The man snorted, shook his head. "These days it does.
Especially with the Ohio elections set to take place here. But
then I guess we likely know your leanings, given your relation to
Mr. Stickney."

Hugh's throat had gone dry as sawdust, his hands wet as
morning dew. And every word he knew fled from his head.

They waited—all of them—as if the success of the newspaper hung on Hugh's answer.

"I—well, I really—" He rubbed the back of his neck,

wishing he'd thought out a response beforehand. But he hadn't. He hadn't seen the need.

Of course, Annis had warned him this issue was foremost on people's minds. If only he'd believed her.

No use regretting that now. He needed words that wouldn't alienate the very people he hoped would buy—and read—his newspaper. This was his defining moment, the one in which he could prove himself worthy of Annis and of the success he envisioned.

He squared his shoulders, took a deep breath. "*The Toledo Herald* intends to serve all the citizens of Toledo, not one side or the other of this debate."

A quiet grumble crawled through the room. Hugh frowned. Not the effect he'd hoped for. He needed to take charge, somehow use this moment to his advantage.

Clearing his throat, he spoke again, raising his volume. "In fact, to demonstrate the neutrality of the paper, I intend to offer the inaugural issue completely free."

The grumble turned to a murmur of surprise. A trickle of perspiration slid down the side of Hugh's face. When had it become so warm in the store? And what had he just done? If he didn't sell some advertisements before they went to print, he'd begin this venture in the hole. Uncle Stickney wouldn't be happy with that. Nor, he suspected, would Annis's father be impressed.

Suddenly the proprietor of the store opened his till. "I'll gamble with you, son, seeing as how you'll have plenty of readers for a free issue. How much for a small advertisement?"

Hugh started breathing again. He quoted his price and received payment as business returned to normal around him. As he moved on to the next storefront, he went with a little encouragement and a lot more understanding. He'd known he had to find news, find advertisements, find readers—but he hadn't realized his biggest task would be to walk the narrow line between Ohio and Michigan.

He repeated the encounter in the first establishment for the rest of the morning, finally reaching the end of Summit Street with a few advertisements but no usable news. There didn't seem to be anything of consequence happening in this town at the moment. Not unless you counted local gossip. Which he didn't. He'd come here to start a legitimate newspaper. If he had to wait for something worthy of print, then he would wait.

Only it didn't seem fair he had to wait for news *and* Annis. After another half hour of sauntering up and down the blocks fronting the wharf in hope of finding news, he slapped his hat against his thigh and headed back toward Swan Creek, toward the edge of the town.

He hadn't passed Mr. Jackson's law office thus far, so the place had to be somewhere in his current direction. Annis had told him she was working there. Likely he could walk by and spy her through the window, remind himself why his success meant so much. Maybe she would see him and come outside.

He turned down Huron Street. It didn't take long to spot Mr. Jackson's name on the window—the letters painted in uniform sizes and even rows—set in a tidy building on the corner of St. Clair Street. Hugh slowed his steps, his heart beating more quickly in his chest as he moved closer to the window. He wanted to stop and peer inside, but that would be too obvious. For now, he just needed a glimpse.

Halfway past the picture window, he turned his head, readied himself to smile in Annis's direction.

Only she wasn't there.

He found himself staring at a desk laden with pens, inkpots, documents, and copybooks.

But no Annis.

Light glowed from an inner office beyond. Was she in there? With her father? Shadows moved through the light, and the sound of raised voices carried into the street. Suddenly a man appeared from the inner office, his back to Hugh, a familiar shape to his body.

Uncle Stickney? Here?

Hugh feared he'd be sick on the street. Had he and Annis been found out already? He stepped toward the door. Perhaps he should. . .

The voices grew louder. Then a larger man loomed into view, his bony finger poking into Uncle Stickney's broad chest, his eyes a familiar shape and hue.

Mr. Jackson.

Hugh sucked in a breath and hurried around the corner, making it half a block before resting his hands on his knees and blowing out the breath trapped in his chest.

Leaning against the side of a building, he squinted up at the waning sun and wondered if heaven was laughing at him. Annis had been so sure of God's blessing on their relationship, especially when he'd told her his uncle had advanced him funds to start a newspaper in the very place where her family lived. How did she reconcile her intellect with that kind of faith?

Hugh had always been a church-goer but didn't hold to a personal God, one involved in every detail of a person's life. God the Creator, yes. But a God who had given humankind the ability to think and expected them to divine their own way in the world. And his way definitely involved Annis.

Yet he found himself wavering, suddenly wishing he believed God would step in and put things right. After all, if He had, as Annis said, brought them together, wouldn't He resolve this issue between their relations?

His stomach growled, forcing his thoughts from the antagonistic posturing and angry voices of both his uncle and Annis's father. Perhaps food would help him settle on his next course of action. Hugh shook his head and trudged toward home, grateful that in his negotiations with Sid he'd offered to share his room in exchange for Sid's handling of the morning and evening meals.

After two long blocks he reached the newspaper office, darkened now. He unlocked the front door and locked it behind him again before striding through the dark room and out into the alley. Light edged the door of the bricked kitchen behind the building, and an unusual smell filled the air.

He opened the door to find Sid sitting on a stool, stirring a pot hanging over a fire in the expansive hearth.

"What are you stewing? Old shoes?" Hugh shook his head, debating whether to draw closer and peek into the pot or not. "You assured me you knew your way around the kitchen."

Sid pressed his hand to his chest. "You wound me with your mistrust. I have a variety of usable skills, one of which is most definitely cookery."

Hugh snorted as Sid turned back to the foul concoction with a grin. "I made a deal with my mother when I was seventeen. I'd cook for us, but she would pay me the same wages she would anyone else. And that is how I cobbled together the funds to travel here. To Toledo. Where I felt sure I could find an opportunity that would enable me to make my own way in the world. And here I am."

Sid's good-natured storytelling loosened the knot in Hugh's chest. He stepped closer to the stove and let his olfactory sense run free. "What is it, anyway?"

"Sauerkraut and sausage. Filling. And most importantly, cheap."

"Fine," Hugh grunted, backing away. He imagined Annis dining on much more sophisticated fare, and it made his mouth water. But soon—hopefully very soon—he'd have invitations enough to join them.

Sid dipped up the stuff onto two tin plates, then set them on a small table against the wall, two ladderback chairs already set at each end. Hugh was thankful for Sid's resourcefulness. And frugality. For while Uncle Stickney had given him the capital to begin this venture, Hugh had no intention of staying indebted long. The sooner he could repay his uncle, the sooner he could impress Annis's father and take her as his wife.

Sid and Hugh settled at the table, Hugh ready to dive into the stinky fare, Sid sitting quietly with hands folded and head bowed. Hugh's eyes narrowed as he put down his fork and bowed his head as well. It couldn't hurt, praying. But his thoughts turned to Annis, not God. Then Sid cleared his throat, bringing Hugh's attention back to supper.

Sid scooped the stringy cabbage into his mouth, then paused. Swallowed. Twisted his mouth in a saucy grin. "A girl came looking for you today."

Hugh froze, fork halfway to his open mouth. He set the bite back on his plate.

"A girl?" He hated that his voice squeaked the question as his face flushed with warmth.

"Seemed like she might know you. Pretty girl, light brown hair all done up in back with curls along the side. And eyes the color of Lake Erie in June. Mmm, mmm." Sid tucked into his supper once more, but his gaze remained on Hugh, sending the temperature in Hugh's face higher than a midsummer's day.

But the longer the silence between them stretched, the more he considered that this might be a good thing. Sid had unlimited optimism and a grand sense of adventure. Even though he'd known Sid only a few days, maybe it would be wise to enlist the help of this enterprising young man.

Hugh cleared his throat. "So you met Annis."

"She came dashing into the office, bold as brass." Sid laughed. "Well, not exactly bold. More like a mouse scurrying to get away from a broom. I surmised she'd escaped from something—or someone—for a few moments and thought to find you here."

Hugh sighed, rubbed his forehead. "Of course she did."

Sid's eyebrows leaned toward his nose. He stopped eating, rested his elbows on the table. "Don't you like her? Because if you don't—"

Hugh's chair scraped the floor, cutting off Sid's words. His jaw muscles ticked as he dumped his empty plate in a bucket of water near the back door. "Annis and I—" He shoved a hand through his hair and sighed. "She was here while I was skulking in front of her father's office hoping for a chance to speak with her."

"Her pa not like you for some reason?"

"I guess you could say that. Though he doesn't actually know me." Hugh sat down again, blew out a long breath. "Mr. Jackson is—well, he's a. . .a . . ."

Sid's eyebrows shot toward the ceiling as he whistled long and low. "A Michigander. And he hates—"

"My uncle Stickney."

As he shook his head, Sid's eyes danced with unreleased laughter. "Even I know this is a bad idea, and I've only been in town a few weeks." He laced his hands behind his head and leaned back in his chair. "So how's it feel playing Romeo to her Juliet?"

Hugh shot up from the chair, paced the room. "We are not —" He emitted a quiet growl. "We are simply two people in love who want to be together. In the end, I have no care whether this strip of land falls to the territory of Michigan or the state of Ohio, though my gut says Ohio would be a better option since it is already well established. We intend to be open about our relationship, but we want to reveal it at the right time."

Sid's left eyebrow arched toward the ceiling.

"After the newspaper has gained respectability."

Sid shook his head.

"After Annis has had the opportunity to prepare her father for such a surprise."

Sid whistled low and long before carrying his plate to the washing bucket. "It'll be a surprise all right." He dunked both plates until they were rinsed clean, then glanced at Hugh again, this time with his face shrouded in concern. "I hope you know what you're doing."

"We do, so don't worry about us." Hugh rubbed the back of his neck. "Although . . . we could use some help."

Sid swirled a drying cloth over a plate and grinned. "Just tell me what you need."

CHAPTER 7

ANNIS HADN'T ATTEMPTED this since she was ten—when she didn't have to contend with a full set of petticoats and a floor-length skirt. But if she had done it then, she could do it now, especially with so much more at stake than a moonlit ramble.

She'd followed through on her plan to see Hugh this afternoon and succeeded only in making a fool of herself in front of his hired man. She refused to let that happen again. In fact, she had no intention of returning home tonight until she had spoken with Hugh face-to-face. This staying away from one another had gone on long enough.

Gathering yards of material into her arms, she eyed the window and the sprawling elm just beyond. She remembered the tree being so much closer than it looked now. Pressing her lips together, she fought back fear. Hugh was worth any hardship she had to overcome to see him.

Annis eased one stockinged leg over the sill, let it dangle two stories above ground. Then she ducked her body beneath the raised window before letting her second leg join the first. Her breath came fast, a mound of skirt in her lap, fingers gripping the small ledge on which she teetered.

She'd also remembered there being much more sitting room than now appeared evident.

But she didn't have to perch there long. All she had to do was lunge forward, grab the large branch connected to the sturdy trunk. She squeezed her eyes shut, imagined reaching the tree, shimmying down, finding her way to town by the light of the full moon.

She could do this.

She *would* do this.

One.

Oh, dear God! Help me!

Two.

Breathe.

Th—

"Annis!" Philippa's whispered cry set Annis wobbling, her heart pounding as she tightened her grip on the sill in order to keep her precarious seat. Then a steady arm wrapped around her waist, held her fast.

"Are you trying to get yourself killed?" Philippa's hiss resounded in Annis's ear as she pulled Annis back inside.

Once back in the bedroom, Annis collapsed to the floor, thankful to be on solid ground, thankful for her sister's impeccable timing. For in the instant before Philippa appeared, Annis had feared she would end crumpled up on the earth, never to rise again.

Philippa shut the window then sank down beside Annis and waited.

Annis sighed, pushed herself up and sat against the leg of their bedstead. She couldn't meet her sister's gaze.

"Whatever made you think you could still—" Philippa shook her head, seeming now the older sister. "Where in heaven's name were you going?"

Annis tried to think of something that sounded legitimate. Even sane would do. In fact, she wondered now why she tried to climb out of the window at all instead of waiting until the deep of night. She couldn't come up with any better story than the truth. The time had come to bring her sister fully into her confidence. She always had before. They'd climbed out the window together as girls, taking midnight romps across familiar landscapes. Never beyond sight of the house, but deliciously adventuresome all the same. And neither had ever breathed a word to their parents.

If her past efforts had proven anything, they had proven she needed help to make contact with Hugh. And who better to help than her sister? Annis reached for Philippa's hand and scooted near, until they sat shoulder to shoulder as they used to do.

"Philly." Annis pulled in a long breath and let her words flow out on the exhale. "I—I haven't been completely honest with you. I've mentioned Hugh—the man I . . . befriended on the voyage home." She chanced a glance at her sister. Philippa didn't flinch or flush, but her eyes went wide.

"What I haven't told you is that I'm in love with him. As he is with me." Annis braced for her sister's response. "And that he is here. In Toledo."

With a quiet squeal, Philippa threw her arms around Annis and squeezed. Then she gripped Annis's shoulders and gave her a playful shake. "But why didn't you tell me the minute you arrived home?"

Annis groaned, laid her forehead on Philippa's shoulder. "I should have told you, I know. Ma and Pa, too." She raised her head, wishing her sister could read her mind so that she wouldn't have to voice the reason for her secrecy.

Philippa frowned. "So why all the secrecy? Is he completely unsuitable? Older than Pa? Oooh! Maybe he's—"

"The editor of the newspaper. Benjamin Stickney's nephew."

Philippa's chin dropped, her mouth gaping for a full minute before she spoke. "Well, I didn't expect that."

"Nor would Pa. That's why it's a secret." Annis looked down at her hands writhing in her lap.

Understanding dawned in Philippa's eyes. "The editor of the newspaper."

Annis covered her face as her sister sucked in a breath.

"What are you going to do? You have tell Pa sometime."

"I know. And we will. But I want to . . . prepare him first."

Philippa snorted. "And how do you propose to do that? You know how he feels about Mr. Stickney. And if this—" She waved her hand as if trying to pull the name out of the air.

"Hugh. Hugh Hylton."

"If Mr. Hylton resembles his uncle in any way, I fear you've taken leave of your senses. Which, I must say, dear sister, is very unlike you."

Annis peeked through her fingers to see Philippa's saucy grin.

"In fact—" Philippa continued as she pried Annis's hands from her face "—this is exactly the kind of muddle *I* usually stumble into."

Annis leaned forward, put her hand on her sister's arm. "So you'll help us?"

Philippa grinned again. "Oh, you know I will!"

CHAPTER 8

Sɪᴅ ᴄᴏɴᴠɪɴᴄᴇᴅ Hugh to relent on his plan to skulk around Annis's house trying to make contact with her. Though she had assured him that her father wasn't a violent man, that didn't mean he might not shoot first and ask questions later if he thought Hugh was an intruder. And he might, if Hugh and Sid appeared under cover of night.

Which had been a totally inappropriate idea in the first place.

But that didn't make it any easier for Hugh to wait. In spite of filling his time working to get the newspaper up and running, without Annis by his side his hours felt empty. Lifeless.

He needed to write to her, answer the one short missive she'd sent to him. But what to say? He didn't see any course of action that wouldn't put them in peril of their relationship being discovered. For a man who excelled at words, his lack of ability to express himself in this moment felt . . .

He let his head fall to the small table, rest on top of the still-empty page, wishing he believed God cared about such a minuscule thing as his note to Annis. He needed some help here.

The kitchen still felt warm, even though they'd doused the

fire hours ago. Suddenly feeling the need for fresh air, Hugh darted into the alley and gulped in the coolness of the March evening. The canopy of stars overhead drew his gaze.

The night sky put him in mind of those nights on Lake Erie, standing at the rail of the steamship with Annis. They'd pointed out their favorite constellations, told each other of their hopes and dreams. Was she looking out her window tonight at the same sky, remembering the same conversations? He sighed, wishing he could feel her small hand in his, her head resting on his shoulder.

"Someone's at the front door," Sid hissed into the blackness.

Hugh sprang into motion. Perhaps something had happened. Something newsworthy. His heart skipped a beat. He swept paper and pen from his desk in passing, his feet keeping time with the staccato tapping on the glass insert in the door.

Sid lit a lantern. Hugh startled. Two faces pressed against the glass.

Women's faces.

Sid pushed past him, unlatched the door. Annis charged through, throwing her arms around Hugh's neck. "Oh, darling! How I've missed you!"

He stumbled backward, one arm clutching her waist to steady them both. She pulled away, took his face in her hands. "How is the paper? Have you found any news to print? I fear my father is already prejudiced against you—and more strongly than I'd imagined!"

A chuckle stilled them both.

Hugh turned to see Sid rub a hand across his mouth, as if wiping away a smile. "Hello again, Miss Jackson."

Annis jumped back, leaving Hugh suddenly cold. He glared at Sid, hoping the boy felt appropriately chastised. But then he noticed Sid's attention snagged beyond them. And the daft expression on his face.

Hugh turned, following the line of Sid's gaze. Annis, suddenly confused, turned also. A young woman—a girl, really

—stood with her back against the door, eyes wide in a round face. She stared at Sid, oblivious to anyone else in the room.

Hugh and Annis looked at each other. *Sister?* he mouthed.

She nodded, her gloved hand stifling what he knew to be a giggle.

Hugh cleared his throat. Sid's rosy-hued face shifted to him.

"I guess introductions ought to be made. To the Miss Jacksons, may I present Mr. Sidney Allison, late of the territory of Michigan. My . . . apprentice—and jack-of-all-trades."

Annis's sister lowered her eyes and dropped a quick curtsy. Sid nodded, his Adam's apple bobbing up and down.

"And this, gentlemen, is my sister, Miss Philippa Jackson." Annis smirked, but then her mouth stretched into an *O*. "We can't be seen! Snuff the light. Quickly."

Hugh blew out the candle inside the lantern, the smell of smoke curling around his nose. Then he reached for Annis's hand and led her through the office and into the alley behind the building. After a moment of relief, he realized Sid and Philippa hadn't followed. They were entirely alone. Even on the ship there had usually been others within sight. Except that one exquisite moment before they'd disembarked. When his lips had found hers.

Before he could turn them back toward company, Annis pressed her mouth against his. "There. Now I feel better. I've missed you terribly!"

Hugh grinned, pulled her closer. Now that he'd had that kiss, he wanted more. He leaned toward her, but his lips found her ear, not her mouth.

"Wait! My sister. I need to get back to her." And Annis disappeared back indoors.

Hugh groaned and followed. The minute he stepped inside, he bumped into Annis. She tugged at his sleeve and pointed to Sid and Philippa still standing near the window, staring besottedly at each another.

"I see," he whispered, trying to sound as amused as she

looked. But in truth, it took every ounce of self-control not to stomp across the room and wrangle Sid outside to give him a stern talking-to. It was difficult enough figuring out how to gain Annis's father's approval. But two couples courting in secret? That would be much harder to conceal in a place as small as Toledo.

CHAPTER 9

ANNIS CLEARED her throat and tapped her foot. It had gone on long enough, this staring into one another's eyes. Even in their days on the ship she and Hugh hadn't acted this foolishly. Had they?

She did remember the teasing looks of a few of the older women with whom they shared a dinner table. Her lips twitched, returning to her earlier grin. Yes, she and Hugh likely had been just as bad.

Still. They couldn't risk being discovered. And concealing her feelings was not something at which Phillippa excelled.

Annis whirled to face Hugh. She ought to chide him for not answering her note, but when she pressed one hand to his chest, feeling its solidness above the steady beat of his heart, only one thought remained in her head. "We need to talk."

Hugh glanced past her, presumably at the inattentive couple, then pulled her close. His lips brushed hers, feather light. Once. Twice. Three times. "Of course. But we should meet tomorrow. You and your sister ought to be at home, not here."

Annis nodded, her stomach churning as she remembered her father's story about Mr. Stickney. How would she tell Hugh that his uncle was untrustworthy? She set her hand on his cheek, his stubble rough against her palm. Yet the discomfort didn't cause her to draw her hand away. At least not the discomfort from his face. Only of the fire now racing through her veins. She took a step backward, afraid of her desire for him.

She had to break the news of their relationship to Pa. And soon. But how? Especially with the added complication of Philippa making eyes at Sidney.

"Do you know of a place we can meet? Somewhere we wouldn't be noticed?" Hugh's voice softened, along with his eyes. He shrugged his head toward Sidney and Philippa. "We could take these two along to chaperone."

Annis chewed her bottom lip, thinking. So much had changed in the two years she'd been gone that she worried she didn't know the area anymore. And her sister would not prove helpful at the moment.

Then she remembered a stand of trees near Swan Creek. As far as she'd seen in their rambles, it remained unchanged. Far enough from town for privacy, but not so far that she and Philippa couldn't walk there and back in a reasonable amount of time, especially from Pa's office. It had been their family picnic spot long ago, but they hadn't been there in ages. She bounced on her toes and clapped her hands noiselessly.

"I know just the place," she finally breathed. "It's about a mile out of town to the south, near Swan Creek, which breaks off from the Maumee River. A ring of trees, presided over by an old oak, its trunk bigger around than you are. We can meet there in the early afternoon, take our dinner *al fresco*."

Hugh visibly relaxed. "The oak tree it is. But will you be able to get away?"

"I'll tell Pa that my sister and I want to enjoy the warmth of the afternoon sun. And I'll have her bring plenty of food." Annis pushed up on her toes and planted another kiss on his lips before crossing the room. "Whoa, Philly." She tugged her sister's arm. "You'll see him tomorrow. I promise."

"Good-bye, Sid!" Philippa called, hand fluttering in a wave as Annis pulled her out into the night. Philippa heaved an enormous sigh. "Did we have to leave so soon?"

"We've been gone too long already." Annis knew her words sounded cross, but who could blame her? She'd taken Philippa along for her level-headedness. To be the one to keep Annis and Hugh from forgetting the time, from being discovered. Instead, she and Hugh had been forced to regulate themselves *and* the younger set.

Annis yanked Philippa's elbow, drawing her close enough to hear the angry whisper. "I brought you along to watch out for me, Philly. Not me for you."

Philippa grinned, skipping to keep up with Annis's pace. "We'll have to watch out for one another from now on, I guess."

Annis splayed her arms in bewildered frustration. "You don't even know the boy! You didn't speak a dozen words to each other!"

"Hugh hired him. Isn't that enough?"

Annis huffed. If Hugh's assistant were besotted with anyone but her sister, Hugh's confidence in him would, indeed, be enough, but she remained unwilling to voice her agreement. "Still. You must be circumspect in your behavior until we know him better. Our picnic tomorrow will give you ample opportunity to practice that—and to get to know Sidney Allison for himself."

As they approached the house, Annis quieted, not wanting to alert their parents of their evening escapade. Philippa eased through the kitchen door first before motioning Annis to follow. They tiptoed up the stairs, shoes in hand, giggles stifled behind locked lips. Once in their bedroom, they eased the door shut, helped each another out of their dresses and donned their nightclothes. Only when they had climbed into bed and thrown the sheet and quilt over their heads did they allow themselves to indulge in quiet laughter.

"Sweet dreams, little sister," Annis whispered before they peeled down the heavy outer covering.

"You too." Philippa turned on her side, hands tucked beneath her ear.

Annis rolled onto her back and stared at the ceiling. She'd worried over Pa's reaction when it was only her secret, her heart and Hugh's at stake. But now that they'd drawn Philippa and Sidney into their deception, she wondered if she'd created a bigger maelstrom by not telling the truth up front and then enduring the storm that would have followed. After all, whether Toledo ended up in Ohio or Michigan, Pa would want their family to remain intact.

Wouldn't he?

CHAPTER 10

HUGH FORCED his mind from the coming picnic with Annis and her sister. He needed to drum up some news stories first, get them written, help Sid set the words in type. And that needed to happen fast. He intended to publish the first issue tomorrow, providing he could find enough news today. And with product in hand, he'd be one step closer to proving himself a man Annis's father would respect, even if they did look at the world from opposite points of view. At least in regard to the governance of this strip of earth.

After a breakfast of passable biscuits and better-than-average eggs made by Sid, Hugh set out. Up and down each street he went, conversing with business owners and their employees, keeping his ear tuned for any hint of news other than the Ohio elections about to take place. That news was on everyone's lips, it seemed.

Mr. Tacker, who ran the bookshop, obligingly gave Hugh access to the Washington D.C. newspaper he received by mail each week. Many residents hereabouts still wouldn't have read the details of the attempt on President Andrew Jackson's life back in January or his continued assertion that the Whigs had somehow induced the man to the thwarted action. He would summarize the *Daily National Intelligencer* article for his readers, use that to draw readers along with election news.

By noon, Hugh had learned of a wagon accident in a nearby town and a new steamship being built in the Toledo shipyard. And he held three advertisements purchased by local merchants. A moderately productive day for having called on almost every businessman in town.

Almost.

Earlier in the morning, he'd passed Mr. Jackson's law office with a quick glance in the window. No Annis sitting at the front desk. No light shining from the interior. Hugh had put his hand on the door and attempted to enter, but the handle wouldn't budge. Locked up tight.

Just as well, for what would he have said?

His stomach grumbled, and the bell jingled as he pushed open the newspaper office door. Sid looked up from the press, gave it one more push, then let it fall still.

"What are you printing?" Hugh waved his hand at their machine.

Sid shrugged. "Just practicing, though it's a bit difficult to gather any rhythm with just one person. Still, I guessed you'd return with news, and I didn't want to lag behind."

Hugh grinned. Over the course of their short acquaintance, Hugh had learned that thinking ahead and aligning the details were Sid's strengths. Which was quite providential, considering that Hugh preferred to focus on the bigger vision, the written word, not necessarily the steps that would get those words into print. Yet another reason why he and Annis worked well together. Like Sid, she puzzled out the small steps that would take them to the final destination.

Hugh hurried through the gate and behind the counter, ripping a page from his notebook as he walked. He held it toward Sid. "You work up this advertisement while I compose my lead story."

Sid took the page, his eyebrows scrunching toward his nose as he considered it. "This all you got?"

"Nope. Two more. And at least a few short items of news we can set in type later today."

"After the picnic of course."

"That anxious to go, are you?" Hugh hid a grin as pink tinged his assistant's face. Sid scowled, then ducked his head, turning to the advertisement details. Hugh left off teasing and sorted through his scribbled notes. It wouldn't take long to put them into narrative form. He glanced up at the clock on the wall behind him, as anxious as Sid to get to see the girls. But even more than stolen moments in Annis's company, he wanted her for a lifetime. And that meant doing everything within his power to create and sell newspapers, to prove himself a man worthy of Mr. Jackson's daughter.

"Go on and wash up," he told Sid a few minutes later. The boy dashed out back while Hugh arranged things so he could easily begin work when they returned. As soon as Sid finished at the washbasin upstairs, Hugh would take his turn. Then they'd be off to Swan Creek to meet the girls.

Hugh's heart swelled near to bursting at the thought of time with Annis. He looked toward the back door, wishing Sid would hurry, but the front door opened instead, snagging his attention.

"Well, nephew, will we see a newspaper in the near future?" Uncle Stickney punctuated his words with a good-natured grin, but Hugh wasn't fooled. A stern businessman looked out from the man's eyes. He might soften his delivery because Hugh was his nephew, but that didn't mean he wasn't anxious to recover his investment.

Before Hugh could answer, Sid appeared. Eyes wide, he looked his question at Hugh, a question not difficult to decipher.

Hugh clapped Sid on the back and led him to the door. "Tell her I'll be there as soon as I can," he mumbled as the bell over the door rang, muffling further the words he had no desire for his uncle to hear.

"Yes, sir." Sid grinned, but his eyes remained worried as he broke into a steady jog toward the edge of town.

Hugh waited until Sid turned the corner, out of sight, then he shut the door and faced his uncle.

"We're just putting together the first issue. It should be available in the morning." Likely his uncle would have heard they'd be giving away the first issue for free, but if he didn't bring it up, Hugh wouldn't, either.

Suddenly Hugh remembered Mr. Jackson's finger poking into Uncle Stickney's chest. He frowned. Annis had intimated last night that she'd learned more information about their ongoing quarrel, but perhaps Hugh needed to hear his uncle's side first. Before being prejudiced into accepting Mr. Jackson's version of the situation.

"Please allow me to show you our operation." Hugh invited his uncle into their work area. For the next few minutes, Hugh explained the workings of the iron press as well as his process for filling the paper with information—both news and advertisements. When he finished, he motioned toward his chair, inviting his uncle to sit, exuding a patience he didn't actually feel.

Uncle Stickney's eyes glittered with something that looked like excitement. "I'm impressed, son. But then, your mother herself has a keen mind. No reason you wouldn't." The man shook his head and sighed, as if experiencing some unseen defeat. "If only my own boys showed such . . ."

Hugh wondered what his uncle might have said. Did his cousins lack something he possessed? Or were they simply stifled by the names One and Two? He pushed the uncharitable thoughts aside, remembering that he'd chosen to indulge his uncle in order to hear the state of things between Uncle Stickney and Mr. Jackson.

"I *have* run into a bit of trouble, sir." Hugh spoke slowly, his gaze fixed on the street beyond the window. The crookedly painted name of the newspaper would be one of those bits of trouble, but he wouldn't address that now. He must focus on the issue at hand. Slowly, he lowered himself to perch on the edge of the desktop, crossed his hands in his lap, and peered at his relation. "There are those who dismiss me out of hand because of my connection to you."

Uncle Stickney leaned forward. "Those cantankerous Michiganders! You can't reason with the lot of them."

Hugh nodded. "But beyond the general opposition, I've come across one who almost likens your name with the devil."

"So you've met Gerald Jackson, have you?" Uncle Stickney chuckled, rubbed his hands together. "You are just the sort to take that man down a peg or two."

Hugh's stomach clenched. He had no desire to humiliate Mr. Jackson in any fashion. And the knowledge that his uncle did caused a burn to start in the middle of Hugh's chest. "How so, Uncle?"

Uncle Stickney shook his head and rubbed a hand over the whiskers on his chin. "We were friends once, but no longer. Not after he refused to see reason and support Ohio's rightful claim to this territory. Instead, he clings the territory of Michigan and its boy governor for no other reason than to make me look a fool."

Hugh returned to his feet, suddenly more agitated than before to get to Annis. "I don't understand, sir."

Uncle Stickney reared back in his chair and stared at the ceiling. "He called me a traitor when I sold out my original settlement claim and moved into Port Lawrence. I only did what was best for my business—and would have been for his, too." He sat upright, his gaze skewering Hugh as if he were Mr. Jackson in the flesh. "I told him this was the direction of prosperity, that we would do well to throw in our lot with the state of Ohio, but once he'd set himself for Michigan, that stubborn man refused to change. And he resented my doing so."

"And yet you both seem to have done well for yourselves, in spite of your differences."

"I suppose." Uncle Stickney stood, slapped his hat on his

head, and strode toward the door. "But he'll have to accept things as they are soon. We're all set for elections—elections sanctioned by Governor Lucas set to take place here in Lucas County, Ohio."

"Yes, I'm hearing that. Do you expect trouble?"

"Of course not!" His uncle stood. "But if those Michiganders have the audacity to try to stop us? Well, let's just say we know how to take care of ourselves."

Hugh gaped as his uncle stalked out the door. Was that what he and Mr. Jackson were arguing over the other day? The coming elections? Possible trouble?

Hugh sighed. He'd hoped this conversation would illuminate the state of things in Toledo, but as he grabbed his hat, locked the office, and jogged toward Swan Creek, he realized he had even more questions than before.

CHAPTER 11

HUGH FOUND the sprawling oak near the creek bank just as Annis had described. Its wide branches shivered naked above a trunk thicker than a barrel. He imagined the majesty when covered with newly sprouted green leaves.

"There you are, Hugh!" Annis jumped up from her seat on the ground and threw her arms around his neck. "I thought you'd never get here." She pulled away, her eyes seeking information in his. "Sid said your uncle stopped in."

Hugh nodded, but before he could elaborate, Annis filled a plate with food—cold ham, beans, light bread, and a cup of water dipped from the bubbling creek. He devoured the food, listening to the others chatter around him. As he finished, Sid helped Philippa to her feet and announced they would take a short walk.

Hugh knew he ought to protest. Annis looked as if she felt the same way. And yet neither of them said a word. They needed a few minutes alone. To talk. Hugh wiped his mouth as Sid and Philippa sauntered toward the creek's edge. Then he put his arm around Annis's wool-clad shoulders, warming to his toes when she leaned into him.

"We don't have long, Annis."

Her dreamy expression turned suddenly serious. "I know." She scrambled to her knees, faced him. "I found out the trouble between Pa and your uncle."

A queer blend of excitement and trepidation raced through his veins. Should he tell her what he knew or listen to her side of the story first? He couldn't understand how a man could rescind his friendship over a line on a map. That decision proved that Annis's father was an unreasonable man given to irrational action. Not exactly a comforting thought.

Annis pressed her palm to his chest. "Apparently they were once allies, both firmly in the camp of Michigan territory. And then your uncle . . . switched sides."

Hugh cocked an eyebrow. Same story, opposite interpretation. How could they bring together two men who each thought themselves in the right?

"Oh, Hugh. I'm frightened." She looked up at him, eyes wide in her pale face. "Pa is so stubborn! Once he sets his mind to something, I've never known him to change. That's why I wanted to be so careful. To introduce you in such a way that he didn't take an immediate prejudice against you." She groaned. "But in spite of all our secrecy, I fear he has already dismissed you—and your paper." She pressed her forehead to his shoulder. He slid an arm around her waist and pulled her closer.

There must be a way—some way—to bring his uncle and her father together, to persuade them to accept each other as honorable men in spite of political differences.

Sid and Philippa returned. "As lovely as this has been," Philippa said, "I'm afraid I need to get Annis back to work before Pa gets suspicious."

Hugh understood the truth of her words, but there was so much more they needed to say. Instead, the conversation silenced as they packed up the hamper. Hugh helped Annis to her feet.

As they picked their way through the tree-pocked edge of

town, Annis clung to his arm, but when the street came into view, she disentangled herself with a sad smile.

"I know." He patted her arm, handed her the basket that held the blanket and the empty tins. Philippa and Sid walked ahead of them, exchanging shy looks and quiet murmurs.

"Annis . . . dear . . ." Hugh pulled her back into the curtain of trees, but the words he needed to say lodged like a ball in his throat. Words to put distance between them until they had the approval of her father. And, preferably, his uncle. He cleared the cowardice and began again. "As much as I love you, I fear we need to do more at the moment than keep our feelings a secret."

"More?" Her face scrunched into something resembling a question mark.

"More. As much as I enjoyed this afternoon, we need to continue to remain apart. Give no cause for misunderstanding or opportunity for discovery. And I need to speak with your father—and my uncle. Me, Annis. Not you." He kept his voice low, desiring none to overhear. He would protect Annis as long as he could.

She stopped, faced him. "But what if he—what if Pa *forbids* us?" Her whispered final words told him she feared this most.

He placed his hands on her shoulders, wishing he could make everything easy for them. For their future. Perhaps he needn't talk to her father yet. Maybe he ought to chat further with his uncle first. All he knew was that he didn't want to distress her. "What do you want me to do?"

"I don't know." Her body trembled beneath his touch. "I honestly don't know. I just want my father to bless our marriage, but I fear his prejudices—" She covered her face with her hands, a low sob reaching his ears.

"Annis." He pried her hands free, tipped her chin upward. "The newspaper debuts tomorrow, dearest." He sighed, gathered both of her hands in his. "I want us to marry. Soon. So either you must talk to your father—or I will approach him, Annis."

"Pray." Annis uttered the word as if it were a life raft in a shipwreck. "We must *pray* long and hard. Both of us."

Hugh nodded, unwilling to rejoin their long-standing disagreement over just how much sway God held in the details of their lives. For now, he'd let her pray while he put the question to long consideration as he waited for her answer.

Although a prayer wouldn't hurt either, just in case.

CHAPTER 12

No, no, no, no, no. Annis paced the block beyond Pa's office as Philippa hopped from one foot to the other in an attempt to keep warm. This wasn't happening. *Couldn't* be happening. God had brought her and Hugh together. Of that she remained certain. So why did He plop them in the middle of such a mess?

A dull pain pulsed across her forehead. She tried to rub it away, but it persisted. What if she agreed Hugh should approach Pa? Annis jerked to a stop, shivered as she imagined their confrontation, imagined Pa telling Hugh to stay away from his daughter.

But the alternative—speaking to Pa on her own—filled her with concern. And no matter who did the telling, would choosing Hugh cause her father to sever his relationship with her, as he had with Mr. Stickney? Then would Ma do? And Philly? Annis blinked back a flood of tears at the thought of running away to be with Hugh, of never seeing her mother or sister or father again. Philippa threw up her hands, eyes rolling toward the iron-gray sky. "Can we go inside and get warm now?"

A sharp breeze whipped past, and Annis shivered. When had the day turned so chilly?

No matter. Philly was right. They needed to go inside. No use stirring up questions from Pa. They'd been gone too long already.

For now, she'd return to her work. And as she copied Pa's words from one page to another, she would pray, just as she'd told Hugh she would. She only hoped he'd do the same. For if she ever needed him to believe God availed His power in the lives of men, it was now.

Several hours later, she wrote her answer and paid the neighbor boy to deliver it.

For the rest of the night, she tossed and turned, wondering if she'd given the right one.

～

"WHERE'S MA?" Annis clapped a hand over her mouth, trying to stifle the words she'd intended as a whisper. If her sister was surprised to see her return home at midmorning, she didn't show it. She simply slid two pans of bread dough into the oven as if nothing unusual were happening.

"She's gone to—"

Annis whipped a sheet of paper from behind her back as Philippa shut the oven door. "It's here!" Annis shook the page in front of her sister's face.

Philly's eyes went wide. She grabbed the paper and plopped into a chair at the small table in the corner. Annis pulled a second seat near. Philippa held the page so they both could see.

The Toledo Herald stretched across the top in fancy letters. Volume I, Number 1, read the sidebar, with Hugh's name as editor occupying the space beneath. Sid's name was there, too. Mr. Stickney's, she noticed, was not. Perhaps that would work in Hugh's favor, in spite of the fact that Mr. Stickney had put up the money for the venture.

Annis held her breath as her eyes traveled over the words again, her pride in Hugh swelling near to bursting. She wanted to press the page to her chest and never let go, but Philippa had a firm grip on the sheet, and Annis had no desire to rip Hugh's grand accomplishment.

"There's a mistake here." Philly pointed to a place halfway down the first column. An *o* that ought to have been an *a*. "And here." Her finger moved to the top of the second column. Two letters transposed. "And here—"

Annis grabbed her sister's hand. "Stop. They've done famously for their first try. Those little mistakes will lessen over time."

Philippa frowned. "I suppose you are right. But they still ought to have someone to proofread their work before going to print." She turned to Annis, eyes sparkling with mischief. "Someone like you."

With a gentle tug, Annis took control of the paper, folding it into quarters and tucking it behind the ribbon that circled the waist of her dress. "Philippa, dear. You know we're already courting disaster even having this in the house. How on earth would I be able to work in the newspaper office?"

Philippa's face scrunched in concentration. "You could crouch behind that counter in the office while you worked." Her expression opened in wonderment. "Or you could dress like a man!"

"Whoa, Philly!" Annis pulled back, as if truly, not metaphorically, tugging the reins of a runaway horse. She shook her head and tsked, until she suddenly realized how much she likely resembled Ma. Then she stopped, settled her face into more agreeable lines. "Hugh will figure out something. But for now—"

The sound of the front door opening stopped her words. She and Philippa looked at each another for a long moment, then they each began bustling about the kitchen.

When Pa strode in, Annis's heart nearly jerked from her

chest. She bit her lip, glanced at her sister. What was he doing here? He never came home in the middle of the day, except to eat his dinner.

Annis turned toward the sink to hide her confusion, the folded page at her waist crinkling as she did. She had to hide the newspaper from Pa or all her scheming would be in vain.

Slowly, she slid the paper into her hand, crushing it smaller and smaller, until she could almost conceal it in her fist.

"Ah. My girls." He kissed them each on the cheek. "It's good to see you together again. And engaged in such industrious-ness." He picked up the coffeepot on the warming burner of the stove, filled a tin cup, then drank it down. "But what are you doing at home, Annis? I thought you were taking care of things at the office."

Annis licked her lips, praying her confusion didn't show on her face. They'd gone to work together that morning, but then he'd left for an out of town meeting, which had left her free to bring the newspaper home to Philly. "I—I thought—I—"

"You know how she loves bread fresh from the oven, Pa. I think she could smell it baking all the way over to St. Clair Street!" Philippa giggled, drawing laughter from Pa, too. And successfully extricating Annis from the uncomfortable line of questioning. Now she could turn the conversation.

"I didn't expect you here before dinner."Annis clenched her hand more tightly around the concealed page of paper.

"Finished my business in Blissfield early, so I thought I'd stop in for coffee on my way back to the office."

Blissfield. A town firmly in Michigan territory. Annis fought a frown. "Did you—" Annis swallowed hard. " Did you finish your business there?"

"Why, yes, I did." He set the coffeepot back on the stove. "A will for an old friend. I'll leave it on the desk for you to copy in the book this afternoon."

Annis breathed out relief. If she could slip away and hide Hugh's newspaper, all would be well.

She took a tentative step toward the stairs, catching Philly's eye. Her sister nodded in understanding as she refilled Pa's cup and kept up a chatter that required his attention. Annis escaped the room, but her conscience pricked. It was one thing to wait for the right time to introduce Hugh to her parents. It was quite another to willingly deceive them. She wanted to be wise, and she also didn't want to sin. Yet as she unfurled Hugh's newspaper and buried it in the treasure chest beneath her bed, she knew she wasn't achieving either ideal.

Perhaps it was time to act. She needn't come right out and tell Pa everything. She just needed to give some hint. Prepare him for the possibility.

She picked up *The Toledo Herald* once more, smoothed its creases as she skimmed the stories. Hugh hadn't written anything inflammatory, only informational. Maybe the newspaper itself would be the open door she needed to win her father's approval of Hugh.

Annis returned to the upstairs landing, listening for Pa's deep voice, hearing only Philippa's clatter. Likely he'd gone back to the office. In another couple of hours, he'd arrive at the table, eat his dinner, and return to work once more. Not until suppertime, at the close of the day, would he venture into the parlor and sit in his chair before the heating stove, pipe in one hand, reading material in the other. And what better to read this evening than *The Toledo Herald?*

If she encouraged him to judge for himself the merits of the fledgling newspaper she wouldn't be *hiding* Hugh anymore. He'd be right out in the open for Pa to see. Then she could suggest they ask Mr. Hylton, newspaper editor, to dinner. As an act of hospitality. As Pa's civic and Christian duty.

Yes. A much better plan than skulking and hiding.

Annis clasped her hands, bowed her head, and said a quick prayer, thanking the Lord for giving her such a grand idea and asking Him to make it all turn out right. When she raised her eyes again, her heart felt lighter than it had since arriving home from Buffalo. A positive sign that she'd done the right thing. Perhaps as soon as this evening she'd be able to deliver another message to Hugh. An invitation. A welcome into their home. The first step on their road to happily ever after.

CHAPTER 13

HUGH STUCK his head inside the newspaper office. "Print more!" he shouted.

Sid saluted as Hugh backed out onto the board walkway with only two sheets of newsprint in his possession—at only midmorning. Excitement shivered up his arms and into his chest as he strode back into the heart of town. Initial response proved the possibilities of making a success of this endeavor. Of course, that could be because of his rash decision to give away this first issue. Which meant he needed to switch from salesman to reporter again. And soon. He had to collect and curate news people would be willing to purchase in time to typeset and print and render the next issue ready for consumption one week from today.

He glanced around, almost expecting to see Annis lurking among the townspeople, eager to witness his success. His exuberance faded a bit when she didn't appear.

At the corner of St. Clair Street, he slowed. The precise and neatly aligned lettering of *Gerald Jackson, Attorney-at-Law* marching across the glass mocked him, but at the moment, readership mattered more than the neatness of his own window. And Annis mattered even more than readership.

So he would beard the lion in his den.

Hugh strode across the street with the confidence of a second printing to bolster him, offering one of his last two papers to a passerby along the way. But he stopped before he reached Mr. Jackson's door. He'd been disappointed in Annis's answer the evening before. *No.* He realized he hadn't been expecting that, yet he'd given his word that he would abide by her choice. And while it still soured his stomach to think of continuing to hide from Mr. Jackson, his euphoria over interest in his paper worked as well as ginger syrup to calm his churning gut.

Perhaps Annis's *no* last night meant she intended to speak with her father today. Perhaps even now, given that the residents of Toledo now held the *Herald* in their hands.

Peering through the window, he looked for Annis. But the outer office appeared dark. Odd. She didn't mention not working today. Or was she too upset to work? Had she attempted to talk to her father? Had it turned out badly?

Hugh sucked in a breath and scowled at the final first-run copy in his hand. If he took a copy of the paper to her father, he would know quite quickly if Annis had presented their relationship to her father. If not, then this tangible proof of his profession would serve as an introduction, a foundation of acquaintance. He didn't have to mention Annis if her father didn't. Not yet. Just initiate a relationship, man to man. Perchance this act of goodwill would put her father in a better frame of mind toward him.

Yes. That would do.

He stepped into the law office and removed his hat, anxious lest Annis dash around the corner and see him.

But he remained alone.

He stood in awkward silence, wondering what to do next.

Then he cleared his throat, hoping that would bring Mr. Jackson to him.

Moments passed. Still nothing.

Finally, Hugh inched deeper into the room, rapped his knuckles against the wall as he called out, "Hello? Mr. Jackson?"

A muffled harrumph gave Hugh confidence to step into the small inner space. Mr. Jackson sat hunched over a large desk, his hair, salted with gray, sticking out in all directions from his head, his dark suit hanging slack from his shoulders.

The man suddenly raised his head. "Gerald Jackson," he said gruffly, remaining seated, his generous mustache twitching over his mouth as he talked.

Hugh surged forward and stuck out his hand. "Hugh Hylton, owner and editor of *The Toledo Hearld*."

Mr. Jackson didn't comment. He simply reached across and shook Hugh's hand before motioning to a chair, lacing his fingers together, setting them on the desk.

Hugh's mouth went as dry as a riverbed in summer, his confidence wavering at the man's lack of enthusiasm. Not impolite or unkind, just not as . . . welcoming as Hugh had hoped.

Maybe this had been a mistake.

But mistake or not, he was here. And if he didn't want Mr. Jackson to think him simple, he had to say something.

Clearing his throat, he tried to summon new courage. Then he remembered the newspaper and extended it with his words. "I wanted to personally deliver a copy of our inaugural issue. Sir."

CHAPTER 14

"ALL DONE, PA." Annis set a stack of papers on her father's desk late that afternoon as he scribbled on another page. Glancing behind her, she bit her lip, thinking again of the newspaper and her plan to give it to her father this evening. Was that really the most prudent course of action? She wasn't sure. She wanted time to reconsider. "I thought I'd run home and help with supper."

He didn't answer. Didn't even raise his head and acknowledge her. Shifting her weight, she wondered whether to speak again or assume he had no objection. Why was it so hard to know what to do these days? When she opened her mouth again, his head jerked up.

"I want to speak with everyone before supper." Then he lowered his head and scribbled some more, but his puckered expression left Annis breathing fast, her hands shaking. Could he have found out about her relationship with Hugh? Or was it something else altogether?

Pa did occasionally ask to see everyone in the parlor, often to pontificate on a particular issue of law or politics, usually precipitated by an article in the *Detroit Daily Free Press*, which he had delivered to him each week. He wanted his girls—Ma included —to be informed on the issues. Thoughtful about the world in a way not usually ascribed to women. It was this forward-think-ing-ness that had allowed Annis—and soon Philippa—to attend the ladies' seminary in Buffalo, the one run by his sister.

Would he have sent her if he'd known Mr. Stickney's nephew lived in the vicinity?

She tiptoed from the room, grabbed her cloak and raced the three blocks home. Then she pulled Philly out behind the house and told her what he'd said.

"Best wait and see what he wants rather than imagine the possibilities." Philippa held out her hand. Annis took it and followed her sister back into the kitchen, the smell of beef stew and fresh bread greeting them.

Together, they prepared supper. A half hour later, Ma breezed in from her meeting at church. They let her know Pa's desire for a family meeting just as the front door opened and closed. Ma hurried to meet Pa in the hall. Annis trembled with anticipation. She grabbed Philly's arm to steady herself, then the two of them proceeded to the parlor.

Pa stood in front of the window facing the street, his back to them. Ma sat in her chair in front of the coal grate. Annis glanced at Philly, who suddenly looked as worried as she was.

"We're all here, Gerald," Ma announced quietly.

It took a few more minutes before he turned to them, a sheet of newsprint between his hands. Annis's heart faltered as she recognized the banner. *The Toledo Herald.* Today's first edition. But its creases from her attempts to hide it were invisible.

Annis frowned, her stomach as fluttery as a feather caught in a whirlwind. Had he taken a copy of his own? And why? It took enormous effort not to glance at her sister.

"This found its way into my hands today," Pa growled, shaking the copy of *The Toledo Herald* in his upraised fist, his face turning red as a roasted beet. "And this is the last time I want to see it in our home." He tossed the crumpled paper into the fire. "Is that clear?"

"Yes, Pa," Annis and Philippa muttered in unison.

"Now, Gerald." Ma stepped forward, curled her hand into the crook of his elbow. He visibly softened at her touch. "Why don't we sit down to supper and discuss things around the table, as we usually do?" With a gentle tug, she led him to the dining room, Annis and Philippa following meekly behind.

Pa settled in his chair at the head of the table while Annis and Philippa helped put the food on the table. When they were all seated, they reached for the hands of the ones next to them and bowed their heads in prayer.

After Pa said amen, the food was passed and plates were filled, but Annis couldn't imagine choking any of it down. She sat perched at the edge of the chair, back straight, feet flat on the ground. As if preparing to endure a great storm of wind without giving way.

After harrumphing and squirming in his chair for a few moments, Pa forked several bites of walleye into his mouth, and his expression returned to its usual placidity.

Ma stirred the boiled potatoes around on her plate, watching them as she spoke. "What has you in such a dither, Gerald? I doubt it is one piece of newsprint, no matter its leanings. Didn't your meeting in Blissfield this morning go well?"

Pa looked a bit sheepish at the question. He devoured a buttered slice of bread in two bites, swallowing, shaking his head. Finishing with a bit of a chuckle.

"You know me too well, my dear," he said with a small sigh.

Annis relaxed a tiny bit. Maybe this wasn't about Hugh—or his newspaper—after all.

"And at my meeting I was privy to some information that has me . . . uneasy."

Annis startled. "But didn't you go to write a will? What could make you—" Philippa poked a finger into Annis's thigh.

They exchanged curious glances before pinning their attention back on their father.

"Go on, Gerald," Ma said. "It isn't like you to keep things from us."

Pa shifted in his chair, and Annis's discomfort returned. Something was indeed amiss. Something important.

"I suppose it's best that you hear it from me. The news will be all over town soon anyway."

News? Annis perked up her ears. Anything that might help Hugh . . .

"Talks have not gone well with President Jackson's men. Governor Mason has ordered the militia to Toledo to stop the Ohio elections." Pa rubbed at the creases on his forehead. "And my guess is that Ohio's Governor Lucas will send his militia as soon as he gets word of Mason's actions."

Annis leaned against the back of her chair, thankful it held her upright. The Michigan militia was practically on their doorstep. And if the Ohio militia arrived . . .

She moistened her lips as she imagined bullets flying, the citizens of the Toledo strip caught in the middle. Until now, it had been only a war of words, not weapons.

"Oh, Gerald!" Ma's eyes looked as wide as an owl's, as if she and Annis were of the same mind.

"Now, Gwendolyn. Don't go making more of this than need be. Neither governor wants blood on their hands. But it will increase tensions among our neighbors. Of that I feel sure."

Tensions would be preferable to someone getting hurt. Or even killed. Was there any way to stop—?

Annis's fear turned to elation. Hugh could intervene by reporting this news. Now. Warn people before any rash actions occurred. Calm them down before the tensions could rise. And establish that his newspaper would support the interests of the entire town, not just Ohioans like his uncle.

CHAPTER 15

HUGH CARRIED two chairs into the back alley, anxious to escape the sweltering kitchen where Sid had cooked their dinner. He sat down and leaned against the wall, balancing the chair on its two back legs. Lamplight shone a dim pathway out the kitchen door, throwing the alley into shadow. Sid joined him a few minutes later and assumed the same posture, no talk passing between them.

Hugh savored the moment, the amazing day. One that portended good things for *The Toledo Herald*. And its editor. He felt the grin slide across his face as he imagined himself wed to Annis, both of them working in the newspaper office by day, enjoying the bliss of married life at night.

Lacing his hands behind his head, he glanced up at the stars brilliant in the night sky. Perhaps this success *was* God's stamp of approval on his work, as Annis insisted. He hadn't thought so before, but he found himself wanting to believe that now.

"A good tired, isn't it?" Sid stood, hands in his pockets, and paced the small area between the office building and the kitchen. "Not just hard work but important work. Something that matters to more people than just us."

Hugh nodded, carefully returning all four legs of his chair to the ground. He hadn't seen this more philosophical side of Sid before. But then, they'd known each other such a short time. "Important work, certainly. But one that affords little rest and reflection. Tomorrow morning we begin gearing up for another issue."

The echo of Sid's grunt of assent died away just as a specter rounded the corner with a swish.

"Hugh!" The voice of his beloved rose out of the darkness.

Hugh jumped to his feet. Why had she come to him? And at night? His "meeting" with her father flashed into his mind and bile rose up his throat. If he'd put her in danger by such a bold action . . .

She stood in a pale swath of light from the kitchen. He grabbed her shoulders. "Darling, what's wrong?"

"Oh, Hugh!" She clutched at his shirt. "Pa told us at supper, and I had to come. He said—he said—"

Hugh pulled her closer and stifled a groan as her face in his shirt muffled her words. No matter. He could guess the issue. He'd obviously made the wrong move giving the paper to her father today. Messed everything up.

Then he noticed a second shadow in skirts. Philippa moved forward, Sid reaching her side faster than a loyal pup. Her face was a mass of confusion, her hands wringing at her waist. She licked her lips, glanced at Sid, then locked her gaze on Hugh. "Did she tell you? She didn't want you to hear it from anyone else."

Hugh's arms dropped to his sides. Her father knew. And he obviously wasn't happy. Annis had come to warn him.

"Annis, darling." He tipped her chin upward, tried to look into her eyes, but she refused to raise her head. "Don't worry. I'll take care of this. I will. I promise." He nudged her chin again, and this time it lifted. He laid a feather-light kiss on her lips before turning her toward her sister. "Take her home. I'll manage . . . something . . . tomorrow."

Philippa gently pulled at Annis's arm.

"And Philippa?"

When she swiveled her head in Hugh's direction, he swallowed hard, unnerved by the fear in the girl's eyes.

"Thank you. I promise I will—"

Will what? What could he possibly promise her? Once more his eyes were drawn upward, to the heavens. If he'd ever wanted help from the Almighty, it was now. He breathed a prayer for wisdom, then pushed his words into the night. "I will make things right. I promise."

When the whisper of their skirts quieted, Hugh picked up the chairs and headed back into the kitchen. Just before he breached the door, he stopped.

"Best get on to bed, Sid. We've work to do come daylight."

What kind of work, exactly, Hugh didn't know. But he intended it to involve Mr. Jackson. Maybe wait at the man's office, bring Sid along to report in case the confrontation turned ugly. For the first big story *The Toledo Herald* reported might just be his own.

THE NIGHT PASSED IN WAKEFULNESS, hours scoffing at his own prayers. God didn't care about him and Annis. Wasn't that the message here? If only he'd trusted Annis's reticence, stayed far from her father until she'd had a chance to pave the way. But no. He'd barged in, brash as you please, and ruined everything.

Just before dawn, exhaustion claimed him. By the time he startled awake, the morning had fully arrived. He threw off the covers, washed his face, toweled himself dry, and hurried into his clothes. After racing down the stairs, he remembered Sid. Then he smelled coffee.

Sid stood in the doorway of the kitchen house, pot in hand. "There you are, sleepyhead. Thought you said today—"

Hugh shoved past him and grabbed a tin cup. "Fill it up. Hurry. We've got things to do this morning."

Sid poured the dark liquid, which Hugh promptly downed as fast as possible without scalding his mouth and throat. Then he barreled into the office to grab paper and a pencil from his desk.

"Sid!" he yelled. Sid popped his head through the doorway. "Come with."

"Yes, sir!" Sid saluted, disappeared, then reappeared again, as jovial as usual. "Where are we—"

Hugh charged out the door, Sid almost running to keep up as Hugh barked instructions. "I'll need you to—"

Suddenly Hugh slowed. As men and women streamed around them, Hugh studied their faces. Some eager, certainly. Others clearly concerned. But the chatter remained lively as more and more people made their way forward, seemingly summoned by some unheard voice.

The journalist in Hugh reared its head like a pointer sniffing out prey in a crowded wood.

"What do you imagine is happening?" Sid asked, hands on his hips as he squinted in the direction of the foot traffic.

"I don't know, but it's worth investigating." He needed to see Mr. Jackson, but Annis would understand his delay. She desired the newspaper's success the same as he. If a story of import to the town of Toledo were indeed taking place at this moment—especially with him in immediate proximity—then he must be there to report the details firsthand.

"This might need a special issue," he said to Sid. "You go back to the office and get things prepared. I'll be there as soon as I can." Without waiting for Sid's agreement, Hugh pressed his hat more firmly on his head and joined the bustling throng, the air charged with anticipation around him. Whatever was happening, it appeared to be newsworthy. And he intended to have a front-row seat to the action.

A few blocks later, the people stopped, piling up like a logjam in a narrow creek. Whatever had drawn them was just ahead.

Quietly, carefully, he eased himself through the crowd, mindful to avoid stepping on feet, muttering niceties as he slid between people. He peered around the heads of those in front of him, squeezed himself closer to the action. Finally, just beyond the wharf, where the streets of town ended, he found an unencumbered view—of the Michigan militia.

Sucking in a breath, he tried to take a step back, but the mass of spectators was as impenetrable as a stone wall. Half a dozen townsmen, all known Ohioans, marched forward. Shoulder to shoulder, chins tipped toward the sky, they stopped a long gunshot away from the men in uniform. Hugh swallowed hard. This could get ugly. Fast.

"We aren't looking for trouble," shouted a stocky Ohioan dressed in the simple garb of a farmer. He punched the stick of his pitchfork into the ground, the tines quivering with the force. "Until *our* militia arrives, which we feel sure it will, be informed that we will be voting in the elections sanctioned by the state of Ohio, under whose jurisdiction this territory falls."

A few militiamen shouldered their weapons. Hugh held his breath until the captain stopped them with a raised hand.

Movement swayed the crowd behind him, like the pull of a wave gathering before breaking toward shore. Voices rose, opponents engaging in a war of words across the sea of people, fomenting arguments among those nearby. The air fairly shimmered with contention. Hugh turned, as eager to see the story happening behind him as the official conflict in front.

Then the mass of humanity shifted in earnest, quiet exclamations of alarm turning louder. Hugh returned his attention to the militia. Mr. Jackson stood near the captain now, his lanky form an easy target for—

A man broke rank with the other Ohioans—was it his cousin, Two?—and disappeared into the crowd. Dismay roiled in Hugh's chest. Whatever his cousin was up to, he sensed danger.

Hugh surged forward, closer to the fray, keeping his cousin

in sight, wary of the anger on his face, the glint of violence in his eye. Instinctively, Hugh looked to the man's hands. The morning sun hit the blade of a penknife clenched in his fist.

What did Two imagine he could do with one small knife in the face of an entire militia? Hugh had no idea. But then his cousin didn't seem to be heading for the men in uniform. His path swerved. Hugh fought to follow.

Until he looked up to find himself an arm's length from Mr. Jackson's back. Hugh stopped, glanced about for a way of escape. Noticed his cousin's lunge toward an unsuspecting Mr. Jackson.

Launching himself forward, Hugh pushed his cousin out of the way, both of them falling to the ground. And then chaos erupted around them. Over them. A hand-to-hand battle, the militia attempting to subdue the citizens. As Hugh did the same to his cousin.

Had Mr. Jackson noticed—either his danger or his salvation?

No time to consider that. Or even to look for Annis's father again. Hugh needed to disarm his cousin. With a quick twist, he wrenched the penknife from Two's hand while his cousin spewed venomous words.

Hugh finally struggled to his feet, pocketed his cousin's weapon and pulled out his notebook and pencil, quickly putting distance between himself and Two.

Behind him, an argument turned into a shoving match. He turned, scribbled descriptions as his attention jumped from scene to scene. Elation over getting a story battled with his concern for these people, this place, what his cousin had attempted to do.

Then a weight slammed into him. A heavy blast of something.

Or someone.

Hugh tipped toward the ground, gripping his notebook,

determined not to lose it. He dropped his pencil, reached out to break his fall. Felt the snap in his wrist just before he crumpled to the earth.

His cry was lost amid the tumult of the angry crowd. Breath surging in and out around clenched teeth, he curled into a ball, protecting his hand—and his notebook. Feet assaulted his shoulders, his back, his legs for a few moments. Then the space around him seemed to expand. He opened his eyes to find several people kneeling over him.

"Are you hurt?" asked a woman near his mother's age, her face a mask of concern.

Hugh eased himself to sitting, schooling his features to deny the pain. But as the woman gently lifted his wrist, already swollen and limp, he sucked in a sharp breath.

"Doc Watson's over there," a man announced before striding away. Hugh tried to smile at the woman beside him but feared his mouth hadn't obeyed. At the throb of his arm and hand, a new worry assaulted. How would he write? Set type? How would he even tie his shoes in the mornings?

With a groan, he shoved his notebook into the pocket of his coat with his uninjured hand. Of all the things to happen right now, this might be the worst. A story—a huge story—and he had no hand with which to write it.

If only Annis were here. She would comfort him, tell him everything would work out for the best. He swallowed down another groan as the doctor knelt and fingered the injury.

"Well, son, you've busted it good." Doc Watson manipulated each of Hugh's fingers, ignoring Hugh's agony. Then he relinquished Hugh's arm, letting him cradle it gently against his chest. The doctor rocked back on his heels and stood before helping Hugh to his feet. "But you'll live. Let's get you to the office and set that wrist so the bones can heal properly."

Hugh nodded and followed, his injured hand pressed over his heart, his good hand clutching the opposite elbow to hold it still. Surely Sid would come searching for him when he didn't arrive back at the office soon. And he wouldn't be hard to find. For everyone in town would be talking about the newspaperman when it ought to be the other way around.

CHAPTER 16

ANNIS PACED the bedroom floor while Philippa sat on the bed, legs crossed beneath her.

"I have to go to him Philly!" Annis almost wailed. "I have to!"

Philippa's forehead wrinkled, her eyebrows scrunching toward her nose as her lips puckered then frowned. "Too bad 'whoa, Annis' doesn't have the same appeal."

Annis blinked at her sister. How could she joke at a time like this? Annis's heart did a funny dance in her chest as she thought again of her prayers, her determination to pave the way with her parents. Was this God's way of overriding her plans? Her mother and Hugh had met each other. Well, not *met*. They weren't introduced. But as Ma related the story of the newspaper man and his injured wrist, Annis had known she was speaking of Hugh. And that he'd been hurt.

It had taken all her strength not to crumble in a puddle at the thought of his pain, especially since her emotions had already been as taut as a laundry line after sneaking back into the house last night. Now Annis needed to find a way to be with him. Care for him. Comfort him. See how badly he'd been injured. And all Philly could do was—

A noise drew Annis to the window, hands and nose pressed against the glass.

"Only the wind, Annis. You're so worked up that Ma and Pa will know something's wrong. Come sit." She patted the empty space on the bed beside her.

With a sigh, Annis did as her sister bid. Philippa put her arms around Annis and squeezed. "I'm sure he's fine. After all, Ma said he got up and walked away with Doc Watson."

"Yes, but—" Annis leapt to her feet and returned to the window, her anxiety shifting into agitation. "Why hasn't he at least sent Sidney to let me know his condition? They could come up with some pretext between them. Couldn't they?" She knew her exasperation was ungrounded but couldn't seem to overcome her emotion with logic. Hugh would come—or send Sidney—when he was able. When there was news to convey and less chance of discovery, too.

"Girls?" Ma called from the hall. Annis whipped around and stared at Philippa as their mother entered their bedroom. "There you are. I've just discovered I'm out of black thread, and your father needs his coat pocket mended before church tomorrow. Would you run to the mercantile and get some for me? Tell Mr. Robertson to add it to our account. And be careful as you go, even if the militia is camped in the opposite direction."

Annis stepped forward first, hands wringing, heart racing. "Of course, Ma." She reached out, grasped her mother's hand, feeling as if Ma had offered her a stack of gold instead of the excuse to go to the store. "We're happy to go, aren't we, Philly?" She turned quickly to her sister, knowing Ma would become suspicious of the excitement on her face over a simple errand.

Philippa grabbed Annis's hand and pulled her into the hall. "Back in a jiff," she called back to Ma as they clambered down the stairs and out the front door.

"Hurry. We have to hurry." Annis's feet kept pace with the thought pounding a beat in her head: *Hugh. Hugh. Hugh.*

～

"Do you think he's still in there?" Annis refused to take her eyes off the back door of Doc Watson's office as she paced near the livery stable. Her nose filled with the pungent aroma of manure —so strong she almost tasted it with every breath.

"There's only one way to find out." Philippa reached for the door handle.

"No!" Annis clapped a hand over her own mouth even as her other hand closed around her sister's arm. She yanked her toward the stable, modulating her voice to a loud whisper. "What do you think you're doing?"

Philippa blinked, pointed behind her. "Going to find out—"

"Why do you think we are back here instead of out on the street?" Annis hissed. Philippa winced, looked down at Annis's hand tightening around her arm. Annis let go, tried to school her voice into forbearance. "Because we can't be seen to have an interest in this situation. Don't you see? Secrecy, Philly. That means other people can't suspect." Annis crossed her arms impatiently over her chest. Sometimes her sister acted as if she had no brain. Aunt Delia's Ladies' Seminary would be good for her.

"But you said—"

"Never mind what I said. What I *meant* was, we'll have to figure out a way to find out. An *unsuspicious* way."

"And quick." Philippa smirked. "For if we're not home soon, Ma will come to find us."

Philly was right. Annis rubbed her forehead, set her mouth in a tight line. They must devise a scheme. And fast.

Never before had anyone been injured in the clash between Ohioans and Michiganders. It had all been only words. So she felt sure the incident would be on every tongue. And second to

89

church, the mercantile was the best place to hear the latest happenings in town.

"Let's go." Annis charged toward the end of the alleyway, Philippa hurrying to keep up. Annis pushed out words with heavy breaths. "We'll go to Mr. Robertson's mercantile for the thread so Ma doesn't suspect we had any other aim for a trip to town. There ought to be plenty of people there willing to talk about what they saw—or what they've heard. Then we can detour by the newspaper office to offer our sympathy and help. Or so we'll say if anyone asks. If Hugh isn't there, we'll wait—or find out from Sidney what is going on."

Philippa frowned. "What if Sid's not there either?"

"Then we'll hide behind the building, out of sight."

Philippa tipped her head to one side and squinted at Annis. "This isn't like you, sister."

Annis stopped, shoved fists to her hips. "What on earth do you mean?"

A slow grin bloomed on Philippa's face. "I mean, you have always been the cautious and logical one, while I, as Pa often says, am 'the soul of adventurous impetuosity.' Acting without thinking, isn't that what you've always accused me of? But since you returned from Buffalo, it's been one thing after another. Is it love that's changed you, dear sister?" Philippa clasped her hands beneath her chin and batted her eyelashes.

Annis rolled her eyes. Philly's theatrics didn't deserve a response. "Are you coming with me or not?" she hissed.

"Lead on, O Fearless One." Philippa struck a pose, as if pointing a sword to the sky. Annis grunted her disapproval and turned her steps toward the mercantile. Philly might find humor in the situation, but Annis understood this was no laughing matter.

As they neared the store, voices carried into the street, the confusion of words reminding her of the cackle of chickens. No doubt each lady inside was boasting over her own juicy morsel. Gossip normally irritated Annis to no end. Except today. Today she was grateful for it, for she needed the information.

Guilt twisted in her chest. Ma would say no amount of need warranted listening to hearsay. Certainly not the *need* of keeping something concealed—especially something as important as the man she intended to marry.

"Well? Aren't we going in?" Philippa asked.

Annis remained rooted to the boardwalk outside the establishment, wishing she knew how to settle the war raging within her. They could go inside and find out where Hugh was and what had happened, or they could turn and walk away—without Ma's requested thread—and return home. But if they took that course, she'd have to spin a web of more lies. And Annis wasn't sure she had the stomach for that.

She turned in a small circle, arms across her waist, fingers gripping her elbows, silently debating. But just as she started her second revolution, finally fully set on a course toward home, someone bumped her. She turned.

"Why Annis, dear! And Philippa! Did you come to hear about the battle, too?" Mrs. Johnson, the young milliner, held a basket on her arm, her eyes twinkling with delight.

Battle? Annis's eyes stretched wide. Was it so bad as that? Ma hadn't made it sound so, but Ma might have tempered the story for fear of alarming them. Wasn't that why she'd come now? To try to discover the truth? Annis chewed her lip, cringed, then nodded.

"Then why are you dithering in the street? Let's go." Mrs. Johnson hooked one arm with Annis, one with Philippa, and they walked in together.

Annis shoved aside her reticence. Maybe this was God's way of telling her she'd been about to make the wrong decision. Yes, that had to be it.

Didn't it?

Half a dozen women stood at the counter, peppering Mr. Robertson with questions.

"Were you there?" asked Mrs. Winthrop, a plump matron Annis had known all her life.

Mr. Robertson scratched his head and smoothed down his hair. "No, wasn't there myself. I was opening the shop. But I got there soon after."

"I heard there were guns involved!" Mrs. Johnson interjected.

Again, Mr. Robertson's hands fiddled with his hair. "Yes, there were guns, but no one got shot."

"But I heard the casualties were taken to Doc Watson's office." A voice from the front of the crowd, a woman Annis couldn't see.

"Well, now, I'm not sure there was more than one injury. Maybe two. I was told that young newspaperman lately arrived from Buffalo got caught in the fracas."

A few women Annis knew—all Michigan sympathizers like her father—looked at one another with raised eyebrows.

Mrs. Winthrop's mouth pursed, as if she'd just sucked on a lemon. "Well, I guess he got what he deserved, then. It's one thing to argue amongst ourselves, those of us who've been settled here for years. But quite another for strangers to come in and take up a cause when they've no notion of its complications."

Annis bit her lip. Her father would feel the same way, she was sure of it. She stepped closer, hoping someone—anyone— would have real information on the state of the injured man. *Hugh.*

"I don't think you have to worry overmuch, Doris," another woman said. "If he broke his arm as my Jim suspects, he'll not be able to continue his newspapering. At least not for a while."

Annis sucked in a breath. She'd been so concerned over Hugh himself that she hadn't considered the larger implications of his injury. If he couldn't continue his work, what would he do? What would *they* do?

Sidney would help, of course, but putting out a newspaper

was at least a two-man job. Or rather, four hands. Male or female didn't matter. Which meant she would simply have to step in and do Hugh's part.

She took one slow step backward. Then another. And another. Halfway to the newspaper office, she remembered she'd left Philly and the thread behind.

CHAPTER 17

HUGH SAT AT HIS DESK, head resting against the wall, eyes closed, listening to the silence. Well, not *silence* exactly. But certainly not the *ca-chunk, clank* of the printing press. The one that should be inking his story about the confrontation between the Ohioans and Michiganders. How the conflict needed to be decided before things got out of . . .

Hand.

He looked down at his sling. He hadn't intended to find himself in the middle of a brawl. Only to see and report it. Instead, he was its one casualty.

So far.

He winced again, remembering the vision of his cousin heading straight for Mr. Jackson. He would have given Mr. Jackson the edge in such an altercation, even at his age, were it not for that knife, small as it was. It might not have killed a man, but a stab wound had the potential to do the same, just over a longer period of time.

He'd reacted without thinking, knowing that if his relations caused further damage to the Jackson family, there would be no hope of a future with Annis. And so he'd intercepted his cousin, wrenched the unlikely weapon from his hand. And ended up losing his own—even if only temporarily—in the process.

If only someone had seen what he'd done on Mr. Jackson's behalf.

Hugh groaned. He couldn't tell the story himself. To do so would be arrogant, boasting—not to mention throwing his family in a bad light. And that might alienate his uncle, who might defund the newspaper.

No. *The Toledo Herald* would not position itself on either side of the conflict between the Stickneys and Jacksons, or the bigger one between Ohio and Michigan. He would write facts. Neutrality.

Peace.

Or he would if he could pen articles to print.

A burst of laughter jerked his head upward, but he kept his eyes closed against the dizziness that accompanied the pain. Sid's hearty guffaw mingled with another—a more gentle, more lyrical laugh.

Annis?

Yet it didn't sound like her. Hugh inched his eyes open to see a woman leaving the shop, a woman he didn't recognize. He rubbed the back of his neck and wondered what Annis had heard. In a town this size nothing remained secret long. It was a wonder their relationship had not yet been discovered by either family.

"Sid!" His bellow startled even himself. Sid appeared in front of him. "Have you—"

The bell over the front door jangled, admitting the very object of Hugh's thoughts. He leapt to his feet and pushed past Sid, every step magnifying the throb of his wrist. Skirting the printing press, he launched himself through the small gate.

"Hugh!" Annis threw her arms around him, the force tipping him sideways. Nothing to grasp near his left hand. His right frozen against his chest.

Falling.

Both of them.

He hit the floor, yelped in pain as she tumbled on top of him, their arms and legs tangled up together.

"Oh, my darling!" Annis scrambled free but remained on the floor. She pulled his head into her lap and stroked his hair away from his face. "I'm so sorry!" She kissed his cheeks and forehead and lips.

Hugh gritted his teeth and fought the fog of pain that engulfed him.

"How badly are you hurt?" Her fingers landed feather-light on his injured arm. She bit her bottom lip while her eyes filled with tears. Placing her hands on either side of his face, she looked as if she would kiss him again. Here. In the middle of the office. Right in front of the picture window.

Hugh struggled to rise. If anyone walked past now . . .

Then Philippa appeared—had she been there all along?—and pulled Annis to her feet as Sid hefted Hugh from the ground.

The moment Hugh found his feet, he grabbed Annis's hand with his uninjured one and pulled her out the back door. Not the most appropriate change of venue but better than being gawked at by any passerby.

He led her to the kitchen and seated himself across the table from her. Perhaps he was being overcautious, but he loved Annis and cared about her reputation, even if she had allowed emotion to temporarily put it from her mind.

"I'm fine, Annis. Really. Just . . ." He glanced at his broken wrist again, then back at her. "Disappointed." With a heavy sigh, he raked his free hand through his hair and realized he must look a sight. He hadn't yet attempted to change out of the clothes that had become rumpled and soiled during the brawl.

Annis leapt to her feet, hands wringing near her waist. "But don't you see? That's why I'm here. To help!"

Hugh's stomach dropped, leaving an ominous emptiness. He needed to explain everything that had happened, including meeting her father yesterday. He chose his words carefully. "There isn't any way you can help, Annis. Not now. I won't further endanger your relationship with your father—"

He shook his head. He couldn't talk to her about her father. Not yet. He needed to make this about himself, not her. About the paper, not their families. "I can't write, and it would take too long to dictate. There will be no articles for Sid to print. We must face the facts, darling, however unfair. I can find another profess—"

Annis stamped her foot. "Hugh Hylton, you will not give up. Not yet. Not until you have at least *considered* a way to keep going."

Philippa rushed through the kitchen door, eyes wide. Her gaze jumped from Annis to Hugh to Annis again as Sid followed closely behind her.

Hugh tried to stand, but the room spun, sending him back to his seat again. He needed to take control. But he couldn't think of the words. Only the pain.

"Hugh, dear." Annis clutched his uninjured hand, commanding the attention of everyone in the room. "Don't you see? I can transcribe your articles and—"

"And I'll help Sid set them!" Philippa linked arms with her sister, the two of them grinning like cats in the cream.

Annis gave a firm nod. "Between the four of us, we'll keep the paper running until your wrist has healed. Now see? Isn't that better than giving up?"

The twinkle in her eye sparked Hugh's hope. It just might work, her plan to save the newspaper—and their future. It just might—

The thought slammed into him like a fist to the gut, stealing his breath just as completely.

"Hugh? What's the matter, Hugh?"

Hugh tried to erase the dismay from his face. "It's a lovely idea." He didn't want to upset her, yet he knew her plan wouldn't work. "But I don't think your father—or even my uncle

—will ever countenance you working here. I've ascertained that my family has the same prejudice towards yours that yours has towards mine." He remembered the hatred in Two's eyes, the small knife in his hand. Hugh swallowed hard, forced himself to say the next words. "Perhaps more."

"But Ma—" Philippa clamped her hand over her mouth, her eyes wide above her fingers.

Hugh sidled his gaze back to Annis. "What about your mother?"

Annis's cheeks blazed bright as a peony in summer. "Well, Ma—you see, she—" Annis's tongue swiped over her lips and her breath came in faster gasps. "She, um . . . Ma . . . was . . . *there.*"

"There? Where?"

Annis glanced down at his bandaged arm. Hugh followed her gaze.

Oh. There.

"And she . . . ?"

"She was with you until Doc Watson came."

Hugh blinked, trying to absorb the new information, trying to picture again the kind woman's face. Why had he not seen Annis in her features? Then hope jumped into Hugh's chest. Hope that her mother had seen the entire situation, could bring it to light.

"So she knows? About us?" He couldn't hide his excitement. His relief.

Annis shook her head. "No, she knows you are *you,* but she doesn't know who you are to me." Annis locked eyes with her sister. "Yet."

Now it was Hugh's turn to groan. He wished he could cover his face with both hands. It was all his fault, really. He ought to have revealed their relationship when he'd first gone into Mr. Jackson's office, if not at the wharf when they got off the steamship.

CHAPTER 18

ANNIS KNELT next to the chair where Hugh sat, her hands resting indecorously on his thigh. "Oh, Hugh. I know I've made a frightful mess of things, but we'll get through it! We will! I have a plan!"

Hugh groaned more loudly, as if she'd knocked his broken wrist again instead of told him she had devised a new way to fix things. Annis rocked back on her heels, then stood, her patience disintegrating like a newspaper left in the rain as she waited for him to look at her.

She tapped her toe. Jammed her hands on her hips. Took deeper breaths. From the corner of her eye, she noticed Philippa biting her lip, then pulling at Sidney's sleeve. The two of them slipped back outside, leaving her alone with Hugh.

Without an audience, her irritation waned. Her foot stilled. Arms fell to her sides. Breath hitched as tears gathered in her eyes. And the moment they spilled onto her cheeks, Hugh had his arm around her, holding her close.

"What are we going to do?" she whispered.

He pulled back, tipped her chin upward and smiled. "I thought you always had a plan, dearest."

Annis giggled. Couldn't help it, really, when he looked at her that way. Then she sobered. Sighed. His eyes looked glassy. His smile, strained.

"You need to rest." Annis pressed a kiss to his forehead, smoothed back his hair. "You've had a trying day, and I'm sure the pain in your wrist will be worse tomorrow. But don't you worry about anything. Philly and I will find a way to help with the paper. I won't let you fail."

Her mouth pressed into a firm line, she led him outside and watched him climb to the second floor. All while her mind raced ahead to what needed to be done in order to save the newspaper and to bring their relationship into the light. If only she could talk Pa around—

Talk.

Aunt Delia had praised Annis's way with words, her use of logical argument in her essays at school. And Pa had long touted her argumentative mind as just what was needed in a lawyer, in spite of her being a woman.

And Hugh needed articles.

So why couldn't they write one? An editorial, actually. About this sending of militias, of escalating the tensions. She—*they* could present the point that they were all part of one nation, even if they were different states—or territories. Like the body of Christ, all had different appearances, different functions, yet all were to work together in one accord. She could persuade the people of Toledo to be more accepting of one another and their divergent opinions.

Pa couldn't disagree with that, as long as she could find a way to make him read it. And she could count on Ma to remind him that the Bible concurred with *The Herald's* point of view.

A grin inched its way across Annis's face. Once she had her parents in agreement with her, she'd mention inviting Hugh to dinner, seeing that they had formed a short acquaintance in Buffalo.

She wanted to run upstairs, tell Hugh, but remembering the

look of pain creasing his features as he made his way to his living quarters, she changed her mind. He was in no frame of mind to make any important decisions right now. But she could get a head start, have a draft ready to show him in the morning.

~

ANNIS DIDN'T TELL Philippa her plan, just curled up on their bed that evening scribbling on a page she'd hidden inside a book. She had to set down the right arguments.

Chewing the end of her pencil, she reread a few sentences, scratched through some words, added others. Soon she would need to light the lamp to see anything at all. But just before she reached that moment, Philippa burst into the room.

"Guess what?" her sister whispered as she shut the door behind her. Annis waited for Philly to answer her own question. Instead, she took her time lighting the lamp, crawling up on the bed.

Annis shut her book with the written page still inside. She couldn't be certain Philly wouldn't mention it to Sidney. Infatuation seemed to have interfered with her sister's judgment over the past few days. And she couldn't chance having her plan derailed.

"Aren't you going to guess?" Philippa pouted, looking much more like a little girl than a young woman.

"I didn't think you were serious." Annis tucked the book and article beneath her pillow.

Crossing her arms, Philippa huffed. "Fine. I'll tell you." Then she softened, leaned toward Annis in their old conspiratorial way. "Polly Mayberry is ill." She sat back, her face alight with satisfaction.

Annis scrunched her eyes shut for a moment before forcing herself to smile. "And that means. . . ?"

"Don't you see? We can tell Ma we're going to sit with her. Or take her soup. Or something. Pa will even excuse you from work for such a charitable endeavor. Then we can go to the newspaper office instead. Isn't that perfect?"

Annis shook her head. "You shouldn't attempt subterfuge, Philly. Not until you learn to think through every detail."

Philippa's crestfallen face made Annis regret her tone, if not her words.

Annis took her sister's hand. "Don't you see? Ma will talk to Mrs. Mayberry, and then we'll be found out. No, we can't use something as seemingly divine as—wait a minute! I've got it!"

Annis scrambled from the bed and began digging through her trunk settled beneath the window. "I had a letter yesterday from Maisy Dickson, a friend from the ladies' seminary. She lives ten miles from here, and she invited me to visit anytime." She shuffled through her correspondence, then held up a sheet of paper with a grin. "We'll tell Ma we'll be gone overnight on the days Sidney needs our help."

"Overnight?" Philippa shook her head. "But we won't be, so where will we sleep?" Then her eyes went wide. "You aren't suggesting—"

"No!" Annis couldn't believe her sister would even think such a thing. But she did have a point. There was a flaw in the plan. Annis paced the floor, her mind racing through several possibilities. Then she remembered the Widow Thorpe, who lived near Swan Creek. The older woman always did have a soft spot for Annis and Philly. She would put them up without an inordinate number of questions.

With a triumphant lift of her chin, she told her sister the plan.

Philippa squealed as she leapt from the bed and enveloped Annis in an eager hug, though whether she was excited to help out or to see Sid again, Annis wasn't certain.

A knock at the door stilled them both. Annis whipped the letter behind her back as Ma poked her head into the room.

"Is everything all right? I heard a commotion."

Annis swallowed hard. "We're fine, Ma. Just . . ." She sidled a glance at wide-eyed Philly, then grinned. "Just pretending, as in the old days. I know we're much too old for that kind of thing, but—" Annis let her shoulder rise and drop again, hoping she looked sincere.

It was a bit frightening how easily she'd learned to lie.

Ma's brow creased for a moment, then settled back into its normal placidity. "As long as everything is fine . . ."

Annis lurched forward, hugged her mother. "Oh, it is, Ma. It is. I'm just so glad to be home again."

Ma smiled at them both, patted Annis on the arm. As soon as she left the room, Annis and Philippa made their plan.

CHAPTER 19

THE PULSE of pain in Hugh's wrist seemed to reverberate through his entire body as gray light invaded his upstairs bedroom. If the discomfort hadn't made sleep impossible, Sid's snoring would have done the trick. Or the remembrance of being awakened by his uncle's face, mottled in anger, telling him to keep to his newspaper and leave the *other things* to those who knew what was what.

Either way, he'd slept little. And fitfully, at best.

Morning light would break soon, so he might as well get up. But as he sat on the side of the bed, the room seemed to tilt. Then his stomach began to spin. He eased down on the bed again, crooked his uninjured arm behind his head and glanced at the shadowy outline of the apothecary's bottle on the small table across the room. One spoonful of the elixir would dull the pain but leave him unable to think clearly. Time had no side effects. Draughts from the doctor often did.

He shut his eyes tight then felt a hand on his shoulder.

"Want some of that medicine now?" Sid asked.

Hugh groaned as he nodded, taking a swig from the bottle Sid put in his working hand. The liquid burned a trail down his throat. Head back on his pillow, he pulled in deep breaths as he listened to Sid bumble around the room in his morning ablutions and wondered how long it would take to feel the medicine's effects.

"I'll set the advertisements this morning," Sid said. "Maybe by this afternoon you'll feel like dictating an article."

Hugh appreciated the optimism but doubted the outcome. Hazily, he remembered his conversation with Annis and pried open one eye. "Is Annis coming to help?"

Sid shot him a surprised look. "She said she'd be here. Philippa, too."

Hugh let his eye fall shut again and nodded, even though the motion made him feel worse. The truth was, Annis could handle all of his intended articles, even scare up some new ones herself. Likely she'd even write them better than he could.

"Sid?" He had to call twice before receiving an answer. "Tell Annis to work up an article from my notes before my injury. And to find some new stories to tell, if she can."

"Yes, sir!" Sid shut the door and clomped down the stairs, leaving Hugh to rest once again. Working together, he and Annis—and Sid—would make the newspaper a success.

HUGH DOZED until a noise jerked him awake. He blinked into the bright room, unfiltered sunlight streaming through the windows. What time was it? What day? His head still felt foggy and his limbs heavy. But at least the ache in his wrist was manageable. Somewhat.

He sat up on the edge of the bed as another loud bang sounded from below. He needed to get up, see what was going on. And why.

It wasn't easy to dress with one hand, but Hugh finally made himself presentable and descended the stairs into the alley between the kitchen and the office. "Sid?"

No answer.

"Sid? What's going on in there?" Hugh eyed the kitchen, knowing a pot of coffee would be resting on the warming shelf near the fire. He needed something hot and bracing. Head-clearing. But before he could command his legs to carry him to it, a rush of silk and lace appeared before him.

"Oh, Hugh!" Annis started to throw her arms around him, then pulled back, eyes wide in her pale face. "You look terrible." She reached up, ran a hand down the side of his face.

He turned, kissed her palm. "I'm fine. Better, in fact. I think." He pulled her to his side with his good arm. She snuggled into him, the tension seeping from her body as Hugh's chest squeezed tight. He loved this woman more than he imagined possible.

A moment passed, then Annis pulled away, clasped her hands beneath her chin. "I've come up with the perfect solution to our problem!"

Eyes bright with excitement, she was an allure Hugh couldn't resist. He brushed his lips gently against hers. Once. Twice. "Which problem would that be, dearest?" he murmured between kisses.

She pressed her palms to his chest, held him away from her, then leaned in close, her eyes staring into his. "Both. We'll write an editorial for the paper, one that appeals to both Ohioans and Michiganders to live with one another in peace, no matter who gains sovereignty over our town. It's scriptural after all, isn't it? Psalm 133 says 'Behold, how good and how pleasant it is for brethren to dwell together in unity.' My father and your uncle will have to concede that point. And I've detailed several other solid arguments in our favor. Once they open their minds to reconciliation, the rest will follow."

Hugh felt his frown before he could stop it. "I'm afraid it won't work, Annis. Not the way you think." He half turned from her, hoping—praying, even—that she would understand the import of his next revelation. "I haven't told you everything,

Annis, about—" He lifted his broken arm. Her pert nose scrunched in confusion. He looked down at his hands.

No, his one good hand.

"Just before I . . . fell . . . I saw my cousin, Two. With a knife. Headed for your father." He shut his eyes now, seeing it all once more. He'd make the same decision, given the chance, knowing he had to protect Annis's father against his own kin even if it meant dissolution of the paper. "I wrestled it from him before he reached your pa."

He opened his eyes to find her face aglow, hands clasped beneath her chin.

No, she didn't understand.

"That's wonderful!" She threw her arms around him. He tried not to groan as her body hit his wrist. "Pa can't help but be grateful."

He took a step back, and her expression changed. "But that's it, isn't it? My father is determined to keep your uncle his enemy. And your uncle—and cousins—so hate my father that one would try to hurt him."

"Annis, I won't put you in the midst of their dispute. I'll—I'll leave here. Start again. Send for you once the fate of the Toledo Strip has been decided. You understand, don't you? I don't want to harm your relationship with your family."

She was crying now. Sobbing, actually. He pulled her into the kitchen house, out of sight of any who might be passing along the back of the street.

"But don't you see?" She pushed out words in between stuttered breaths. "The editorial will help with this division in our families. It will. I'll make sure Pa reads it, and of course your uncle will, too. Then you can come to the house and meet Pa and—"

"I've met him." The words emerged quiet and raspy.

Annis's mouth dropped open. "You . . . what?"

Hugh cleared his throat, suddenly feeling as traitorous as Two Stickney. "I went into his office and gave him an inaugural issue of the paper." He watched his finger trace a circle on the table top, unable to look at Annis's face, to see her reaction.

"*You* did that. He had *your* copy." Her words came out strangled. Stiff. "What did you say to him?"

Hugh looked up. "Nothing. In the end, I said . . . nothing."

Annis's dainty lips pressed into a hard line, her chest rising and falling with each breath. "Why didn't you tell me?" The words were clipped. Almost angry. She'd never spoken to him that way before. He didn't like it. He didn't like it at all.

He reached for her again, but she scooted away. He frowned, trying to figure out how to make amends. Maybe he should let her write that article, even if he had no intention of printing it. As he fought for reason through the haze of pain and medication, Annis's face softened, her arms dropped to her sides. She stepped forward, rested one hand gently on his arm.

"You look pale, darling. Why don't you rest? Sid and I have things in hand. By this evening, we'll be ready to print the special issue."

Hugh nodded, his knees suddenly weak, his wrist throbbing. She helped him up the stairs, to his bedroom. A highly inappropriate action, but one he had no power to stop. He sank down on the edge of his bed as Annis picked up the bottle of medication. She filled the bowl of the spoon and held it out to him. He drank it down.

"Now rest," she said, gently pushing him to lie down. "I'll do my best for the paper. And for us. I promise."

Hugh relaxed. He could count on Annis to keep her word.

CHAPTER 20

ANNIS SCRIBBLED out a short article about a new shipment of fabric available at the mercantile to fill in around the advertisement and the longer article about the clash of militia and townspeople. Meanwhile, Philippa helped Sidney set the type, both girls ducking behind the counter when Sidney spied someone within view of the large front window. Which meant they didn't work as quickly as they would have liked.

But by the time the girls returned home later that afternoon, their story rehearsed to perfection, little remained to be done in order to have the paper ready to sell the next morning.

After supper, Annis and Philly joined their parents in the parlor, Ma knitting while Pa read his paper. The Michigan one, not Hugh's. Philippa kept them entertained with light-hearted pieces on the piano.

Hugh had declined the idea of an editorial. And she had acquiesced, not wanting to burden him further. But the idea hadn't left her mind. In fact, her surety in the soundness of her idea had only grown.

What if . . .

She tapped the pencil against her closed lips, gaze racing around the room, settling on nothing.

What if she wrote it anyway? Sneaked back to the office when her parents imagined her in bed? If the story appeared in the paper without his knowledge and didn't provide the town—and her parents—the soothing balm she imagined, he could truthfully say he had nothing to do with it.

She'd have to leave Philly behind. She couldn't chance any suspicion. Or detection. Once her sister was sleeping, she could tiptoe out of the house. One glance beyond the glass assured her the moonlight would illumine her way through the streets, which would be empty at that time of night.

If only she could figure out a way to get into the newspaper office without exciting suspicion.

During Sidney's quick tutorial that afternoon on how a newspaper comes into being, it had become abundantly clear to Annis that the printing process was, indeed, a two-man job. In spite of Sidney's determination to do whatever was required to get the articles set and the pages inked, it would be almost impossible for him to do alone, even if Hugh managed to lend his one good hand. Which he likely couldn't do if he'd continued to use Doc's medicine to douse the pain in his wrist.

She could help Sidney run a proof copy of what they'd finished earlier and offer to proofread it while Sidney took a catnap. Then she could set her editorial in type herself. When he came down later to run the plates after she inked them, no one would be the wiser.

Once her article appeared, once Pa and Ma and Mr. Stickney and his sons read it and concurred, then Hugh would be pleased. Elated, actually. Their way would be smooth before them, as was always meant to be.

Annis chewed on the end of her pencil, her diary open on her lap. Thanks to both her natural inclinations and her training at the ladies' seminary, she knew how to put her thoughts into words. And so she simply wrote, feeling again the rightness of her words in the eyes of God. All while the rest of the family remained oblivious to her task.

As she finished, excitement buoyed her from her seat. The moment she stood, Philly's music ceased, Pa looked up from his paper, and Ma's knitting needles stopped clacking. All eyes locked on Annis.

"I'm awfully tired." She tried to yawn but feared she looked like a gaping fish instead. "I think I'll trot off to bed now."

Philippa's forehead wrinkled in confusion, as she were if trying to figure out Annis's plan. Then she stood, too. "I'll retire as well."

Annis tamped down her irritation as she kissed first Pa, then Ma on the cheek and bid them good night. Philippa hurried after her up the stairs.

"What's the matter?" Philippa whispered as soon as they were behind their closed door.

Annis kept her eyes averted as she began to remove her clothing. "Like I said. I'm tired."

This part would be the hardest. Dressing quietly. In the dark. Staying clothed would raise too many questions. And going out in her nightdress wasn't an option.

"Really?" Philly plopped onto the edge of the bed, a pout on her full lips. "I thought you might be planning to go back to the newspaper office."

Annis's heart crawled into her throat. She turned away from her sister and slipped into her nightclothes without loosening her corset, hoping Philippa hadn't noticed. It would save a little time later, and the discomfort of it would keep her from falling asleep.

"Why would I go back tonight? Sidney will manage, even if it takes him all night. We can check on his progress in the morning." Annis shimmied beneath the covers.

"I suppose you're right." Philippa began her nightly routine as Annis shut her eyes and regulated her breathing, hoping her playacting of sleep was more convincing than that of being tired.

The room quieted and grew dark. Pa's heavy footsteps and Ma's lighter ones climbed the stairs. Their bedroom door closed, silencing the quiet murmur of their voices.

After some fitful tossing and turning, Philippa stilled, too. Annis counted slowly to one thousand before easing from bed, fumbling into her clothes, tiptoeing down the stairs and out the door.

Thankful her moonlit path led in the opposite direction from the camped militia, Annis reached the office in record time, relieved to see a lamp still burning and Sidney hard at work. Through the window she spied him rubbing his eyes. Yes, he was tired. She'd make sure they ran a proof copy then send him for a quick nap, assuring him she'd make the necessary changes. Easy breezy.

Annis knocked lightly on the window. Sidney startled, blinked at the window. Could he see her? She reached the door at the same time he opened it.

"Annis! I wasn't expecting you back." Sidney hurried her inside, glancing up and down the street before barring the door and pulling her into the shadowy recesses of the room.

She removed her gloves, set them on Hugh's desk. "And how would you have run the press alone? Hmm?"

"I, uh . . . " Sidney set his hands on his hips, let his head hang. He whooshed out a big breath, then raised his gaze to her again. "Slowly. And not very well."

Annis grinned, giving him a curt nod. "Exactly as I suspected. Now, show me what you've done and we'll get to work."

A little while later, a series of yawns nearly split his head in two. Annis laid a hand on his shoulder. "We've got a good print. I'll check it for errors while you rest. I'll come for you when I'm finished, then we'll run all the copies."

Sidney began to protest, but another yawn cut off his words.

He rubbed a hand down his face and shook his head, as if trying to force himself awake.

"Go on," Annis urged. "I'm fresh as a daisy. And just think how pleased Hugh will be in the morning to learn we've finished the job!" Annis followed Sidney into the alley, urging him toward the kitchen, for she knew he wouldn't trust himself to lie in bed. Truly, the thought of Hugh's relief that the paper would go out on time had bolstered her energy and firmed her resolve.

The soft click of the kitchen door signaled her return to the office. She brightened the kerosene lamp on the table as much as she dared, praying no one was prowling the streets in the middle of this night. At least no one who would notice that the shadow in the newspaper's office was more shapely than Sidney or Hugh.

Pulling a paper from the bodice of her dress, she unfolded it and read it again, careful to look for holes in her logic. Satisfied, she removed the words asking for information about Mr. Sweeney's missing cow and reset the letters to reflect her own thoughts. At the end, she hesitated. She couldn't sign her own name, that was obvious. But should she leave it to be assumed as Hugh's doing?

Perhaps a pseudonym would be best.

She tapped a pencil against her lips.

What about Toledo as a surname? As if the town itself were pleading with its people. And she could reverse her own initials at the beginning.

J. A. Toledo. That would work. It sounded masculine. Authoritative. And hopefully unidentifiable.

But would it all be enough? Would it heal the rift between their families? Pave the way for her future with Hugh?

Only time would tell.

Her task complete, she slipped across the alley, into the kitchen, and shook Sidney awake. They worked together, Annis inking the tray, Sidney placing the paper, pulling the handle, and hanging the finished product to dry.

An hour before dawn, Annis scooted out the back door and made the more perilous trip through town, into the house, up the stairs, and into her bedroom.

Philippa stirred as Annis reached bed once again, hastily clad in nightclothes.

"What's the matter?" Philly mumbled.

"Chamberpot," Annis whispered.

Philippa grunted, turned over, and returned to sleep.

Annis, on the other hand, lay grinning into the darkness, thanking God that He'd given her success. For if such a plan had appeared in her head and then gone off without a hitch, it had to have come from Him.

CHAPTER 21

HUGH WOKE to the chirping of birds and the dawn of a new day. When he sat up, he noticed less pain in his wrist and a clearer head. That was good, at least. As for the paper . . .

Slowly, he recognized the thump of the rounce carrying the bed of the press beneath the platen. He imagined Sid pulling the lever, making the impression of the typeset words. But was he down there trying to do it alone?

Hugh intended to wash and dress as quickly as he could with one workable hand, his only thought to help Sid and save the newspaper, but his glance caught on the proof copy of the paper on the table. He picked it up and hurried down to the office, where he no longer heard the *ca-chunk* of production.

When he walked in, Sid was actually pulling down dry papers and stacking them on the counter.

"You didn't wait for me to look over the proof?"

Sid turned to him with a grin. "Annis was here last night. She did it."

Hugh hesitated, uneasy. Because Annis had been here and he hadn't known it? Or because he worried she hadn't done as thorough a job as he would have?

But that was silly. Annis excelled in every subject at the ladies' seminary—from geography to philosophy to rhetoric. To doubt her would be to claim superiority of mind and education, which in his heart he knew wasn't true. And a newspaper man ought to be committed to telling the truth.

He groaned and dropped into the chair behind his desk. What good was telling the truth to himself or the public if he couldn't expose his true feelings for Annis to her father?

No longer in pain, no longer befuddled by the draught from Doc Watson, Hugh chastised himself for his wrongs, determined to put them right. To do so before Annis had a chance to talk him out of it again.

As Sid continued to stack the finished papers, Hugh firmed his resolve. Then his stomach growled. Loudly. So loudly that Sid peeked at him, a look of apology on his face.

"Sorry I didn't make breakfast this morning. I've been—" He glanced at the press.

"I know. I appreciate your work. Why don't I nip across to the hotel and get us some breakfast?"

Sid cocked one eyebrow. "And you'll carry it back here how?" His pointed look landed on Hugh's wrapped arm.

"Oh." Hugh's shoulders sagged. Helplessness was not a state he excelled in. Then he remembered a basket in the kitchen. Yes, that was it. He might be down an appendage for the moment, but his brain had returned to fine working order. He'd ask Mr. Garland to fill the basket, promise him a free issue of the special edition in addition to the fee.

Problem solved.

Hugh returned a half hour later. After he and Sid had filled their bellies, Hugh grabbed a stack of newspapers. "I'll distribute. You've done more than your fair share already."

Sid started to protest, but Hugh jumped in again. "I'm feeling much better, and it will do me good to get outside. Besides, nothing is wrong with my legs. Or my mouth." Hugh grinned, relieved to once again be of some use. He hurried away before Sid could think of another reason why he couldn't.

He stopped first at the hotel, put the page into Mr. Garland's hands personally, then left a stack at the front desk for the man to sell to guests and other visitors. After that, he slowed his pace. Yes, he'd wanted to breathe fresh air. To exercise his stiff limbs. But even more he wanted to see Annis's father. He couldn't decide if he wanted to get a glimpse of her or not. On the one hand, the sight of her face would grow his courage. On the other, she would likely try to stop him. And whether or not she agreed, he would speak with her father—today.

~

AFTER SELLING ALL the copies he carried, Hugh decided to stop in and check on things at the office before visiting Mr. Jackson. He walked down St. Clair Street, rehearsing what he'd say. Lost in his thoughts, he didn't see his uncle loitering in the doorway of the newspaper office until he blocked Hugh's path.

Unease slithered through him. His paper was more popular today than last week. He uncle ought to be here to congratulate him, but he feared this was not the case. Still, he could attempt to sway the situation.

Hugh's mouth tugged upward. "Hello, Uncle. I hope you—"

Uncle Stickney grabbed his good arm and marched him around the back of the building.

"What do you mean, taking me to task like that? Have you no shame? You'd not be here at all if it weren't for my money. And my influence!" He gave Hugh a small shake.

Hugh glanced at the door leading into the office from the alleyway. It inched open, Sid's ashen face visible in the crack.

Hugh frowned. What in the world was his uncle talking about? He hadn't taken anyone to task. In fact, he'd specifically chosen not to write anything personal about the "incident," feeling that his position as victim and editor constituted a conflict that would do his paper no good in terms of circulation. He remembered scribbling a specific note to Annis to leave that part out. So why—

"J. A. Toledo." Uncle Stickney spat the name. "As if anyone can't figure out it's you. I forbid you to print any more of these high-handed judgments or I will pull all my support, financial and otherwise."

J. A. Toledo?

Annis.

Hugh schooled his features to remain neutral as Sid stepped into the alley, his face red as a ripe tomato. Any second now, steam would shoot from the boy's ears.

"Do you have a copy of this issue, Uncle?"

"Of course not," he spat. "I ripped it in two and threw it in the fire. As, I imagine, did everyone else—both Ohioans and Michiganders!"

Hugh fought a smile. Without yet understanding why, his paper had apparently accomplished the impossible—bringing both sides in agreement over something.

Sid thrust a copy in Hugh's hand. Hugh scanned the page.

There. Top center. He began reading.

Earlier this week, an incident occurred which brought our community into an atrocious light. . . . People not inclined to live out the admonitions of Scripture . . . A lack of respect for one another and society . . . A situation ripe for violence . . .

He shot a glance at Sid, whose face remained a mass of anger and confusion. Clearly he hadn't been an accomplice. She'd done this all on her own. In an attempt to help him, probably. And while she'd created a modicum of unity with her words, she'd also stirred a firestorm he didn't know how to quench—not without killing her love for him or his business. He didn't think he could save both.

He needed time to figure out the next step, to calm things until then. On impulse, he folded the page and ripped it in half.

"As editor, the content of my paper *is* ultimately my responsibility. I apologize for the tone of the article by—er—Mr. Toledo."

Uncle Stickney's face relaxed a little. Hugh's anxiety eased. For a moment. Then it rose more fiercely than before. He would not allow his uncle to assume he could dictate Hugh's thoughts, his freedom of speech. Hugh raised his chin, looked his uncle square in the eyes. "But know, Uncle, that I do not apologize for its substance."

For all her impetuousness, Annis was ultimately right. This rancor between Michiganders and Ohioans was quickly reaching the boiling point, all due to the actions of the governors of those two places. In truth, the boundary would ultimately be settled, the maps drawn, in Washington, D.C. Then the citizens populating this disputed strip of land would have to decide to leave or to stay.

But that opinion wasn't popular here. Mr. Jackson likely would disagree with him, just as his uncle did.

What was it St. Paul had told Timothy in Scripture? Not to let his youth be despised? He'd also said, Hugh remembered, for younger men to speak to elder men with respect.

Hugh pulled back his shoulders and softened his tone. "We do, indeed, need a new understanding between us. A solidarity among the residents of Toledo that transcends territorial loyalties."

Hugh raised a hand as his uncle looked ready to explode. "But again, I apologize for the tone of this particular piece. And while I assure you that I, as reporter and editor of *The Toledo Herald*, will publish the facts, I will also allow others to state their own opinions, even if they differ in part or whole from my own."

Uncle Stickney didn't look happy, but at least he didn't seem ready to abandon Hugh and the newspaper altogether.

For now.

When Uncle Stickney stalked away, Sid and Hugh returned to the office interior. Sid plopped into a chair, shoulders slumped, head held in his hands. "I don't know what happened. I set the type and ran the proof copy myself." He looked up, agony clear on his face.

Hugh clapped Sid's broad shoulder. "It wasn't your fault."

Sid hopped up, arms spread wide in frustration. "But how— Oh." He dropped into the chair as if the weight of understanding had pressed him there.

Hugh cleared his throat, looked away. While he'd gladly lose the newspaper to keep Annis's love, losing the newspaper meant losing the ability to provide for her, to be with her forever. In her desire to hurry up that hoped-for day, she might have destroyed that dream altogether.

Clearly, this situation would require wisdom he didn't possess to put things right. Wisdom he had no idea how to procure. Not unless Annis was right in her belief that God desired to intervene in personal affairs and decisions. The only option he had was to pray as he had never prayed in his life and trust that if God had any interest in the details of his life, He would provide an answer.

CHAPTER 22

"WHAT HAS you looking as happy as a honeybee in spring?" Philippa crossed her arms, leaving Annis blinking in surprise as the cup she'd just washed and held out to her sister to dry dripped water on the floor between them.

Philippa raised her eyebrows, looked to the growing puddle then back at Annis. Annis frowned, set the cup on the table, then stooped to wipe the floor. Pa had returned to the office after their midday meal, but Annis had stayed behind. To help clean up, she'd told him. But really to give herself time to saunter through town listening for responses to her article.

"I don't know what you mean." Annis stayed on her knees, hunting the floor for any stray droplet to capture.

"Oh yes you do, sister dear." And suddenly Philippa was cupping Annis's shoulders, pulling Annis to her feet. Linking their arms, Philippa led them out the back door, away from the house. "I don't intend to be left in the dark!" Her whisper pierced Annis with guilt.

She had been proud of herself for keeping her secret. Apparently so proud it showed. She sighed, praying Philly was her only miscalculation. She needed her plan to work, to not only turn her parents' thinking but to boost Hugh's overall business. To hasten the day when she could call herself Mrs. Hugh Hylton.

When they'd walked beyond the privy, Philippa stopped and crossed her arms once more. "Now tell me"—she leaned closer to Annis in spite of their isolation—"did you and Hugh elope?"

Annis's mouth dropped open. Clearly she would have to apprise her sister of the real situation.

"Absolutely not!" Annis kept her voice low as her pace took them quickly toward the cover of a stand of trees at the edge of their property. "How could you even—I would never disgrace our family like that."

Stopping in the leafy shade, Annis faced her sister and let her volume return to normal. "Nor would I forfeit the day of public happiness when we are united in marriage."

Philippa's face scrunched into a dramatic pout. "Oh."

Annis huffed, inexplicable tears rushing into her eyes. Moments ago her plan had seemed genius. Foolproof. But suddenly the thought of saying the words out loud revealed a taint not visible before. Like rust discovered at the bottom of one's drinking cup. She hugged herself tightly. Her bottom lip quivered. She stilled it with her teeth.

"Oh, Annis! What's happened?"

A tear slipped down Annis's cheek. Then another. And another.

"Oh, Philly!" She threw her arms around her sister and sobbed into her shoulder. "I think I've made a terrible mistake!"

THEY WALKED BACK to the house together, Annis's face washed clean of tears. But how to explain her lengthy absence to Pa? Philippa assured her they would manage, but Annis had now lost all taste for falsehood. None of this would have happened if she'd listened to Hugh. He'd wanted to meet her parents right off, gain their trust over time. But she'd persuaded him otherwise. As if her parents were ogres who would lock her in an impenetrable tower.

What had she been thinking?

She hadn't. That much was clear. After two years of education, she was an even bigger dunderhead than before. At least when it came to common sense.

They were almost at the threshold of the house when Annis stopped. "I think I need to take care of something first." She could see the church steeple just over the rise. She needed its solitude, if only for a moment.

Philippa squinted. "What are you—?"

"Don't worry. I'm not going to do anything stupid." She squeezed her sister's arm. "I promise. I just need a few minutes alone."

Philippa nodded. "But hurry back. I expect Pa will be anxious, and I can only cover for you for so long."

"I know." She kissed her sister's cheek and took off down the road, toward the church. She hadn't given the Lord her undivided attention since—

If she were honest, since the trip across Lake Erie with Hugh. How quickly she'd slipped down a slope of lies since then. She'd told herself it was because she loved him so much. But maybe it was because she didn't trust God enough. She who had insisted that God loved and cared for every detail in their lives.

Whatever the reason, falsehood had become a disease in her soul. And the only cure was a repentant heart. One determined to make right her wrongs, even if the consequences hurt.

She would spend a little while in quiet prayer, then she would tell her parents the entire truth.

CHAPTER 23

HUGH HAD TO CONFRONT ANNIS.

After an entire afternoon of pacing and praying, of searching the Scriptures, of wrestling with his conscience, with God's approval—or not—of his behavior, he'd come to see God truly cared that Hugh spoke and acted in truth. And only in honesty could he find any modicum of peace. A deep, inner peace that could only come from something—Some*one*—outside of himself, of his own desires.

Only in the truth could he and Annis hope to find a happy ending.

He'd start by admitting his own faults in the matter with Annis—not meeting her father immediately, in spite of her reticence. Not facing his uncle with his cousin's attempted misdeed.

Not standing his ground regarding what was right and true.

But would admitting his part in each fiasco be enough? Would it foster in Annis an understanding of her wrong as well?

He wished he could be sure. For as much as he loved Annis, he had come to recognize her quiet will of iron. Which could be good.

And not so good.

Hugh dressed in his best suit, the one he'd worn the night he'd first laid eyes on her, felt the first spark between them at a dinner party in Buffalo. The one he wore again during their time on the *Cleveland*. But whatever her response, he intended to put things rights with her father. Assuming he and Annis still had a relationship after he said his piece.

Stepping into the newspaper office, he found Sid busy printing his response to J. A. Toledo's editorial. It had been difficult to compose, for in the end, Annis was right. They needed to help each side see they had more in common with one another than the state or territory with which they'd each aligned themselves, for the prosperity of the Toledo Strip affected them one and all. And yet the tone of her words, the arrogant chastisement that was now attributed to him by his readers—for that he had written an apology.

Sid set down the ink balls. "You're off, then?" With the back of his arm, he wiped sweat from his forehead.

"After I get help with—" Hugh flipped the ends of his cravat. Sid wiped his hands on his leather apron before yanking on Hugh's tie. "Egads! Don't choke me to death!"

Sid laughed, loosened the knot, then stepped away. "I'll try not to get you and Philippa mixed up in this mess, but I can't guarantee anything." He meant the sentiment, in spite of his gruff words.

"I know." One corner of Sid's mouth tugged downward in disappointment, but it rose again just as quickly. "Don't be too hard on Annis. You know she did it for you."

Hugh gave a sharp nod. "I know." Proceeding through to the front door, he felt his resolve quiver. He turned back, waited for Sid to look in his direction. "Pray for me, will you?"

Sid grinned. "Don't worry. I may not have known much about printing when I met you, but I've always known how to pray."

Hugh continued out the door, grateful for the breeze that

cooled his heating face. Now if only the walk to Mr. Jackson's office would still the jangle of his nerves.

~

STOPPING ON THE CORNER, well before he'd be spotted from the law office, Hugh suddenly reconsidered his plan to talk with Annis first. Maybe he ought to simply walk through and address her father. After all, he and Annis wouldn't be able to have a private conversation right there in front of the picture window, her father only a flimsy wall away.

A scowl crawled over his face. He'd come with the express purpose of setting everything out in the open, so why did he now cower at the prospect? Truly, he needed to buck up, be a man. Even if it meant losing Annis. For he couldn't love her the way she deserved to be loved if he lost his self-respect.

Fortifying himself with a deep breath, he turned and marched past the law office window, put his hand on the front door, and turned.

Locked.

He frowned, peered through the glass.

No lights lit. Not even a glow from beneath Mr. Jackson's inner office door. Where were they? He expected them to be here, at work. Had they quit early?

Hugh ran his hand through his hair, let out a frustrated huff. If they'd gone home, then he'd find them there.

A few blocks later, he trudged up the front steps of the Jacksons' home, rapped on the door, and prayed Annis answered the summons. Before the echo faded, the latch turned, the door opened, and he stood face-to-face with the woman who'd helped him when he broke his arm.

Annis's mother took a step back, startled, it seemed, to see him there.

Hugh swiped his hat from his head. "Excuse me, Mrs. Jackson, but might I be permitted to speak with your daughter?"

The moment her eyebrows crunched in confusion, he clarified. "Annis. I wish to speak with Annis."

"Of course, Mr—?" She swung the door wide even as she asked.

"Hylton, ma'am. Hugh Hylton. We met when . . ." He lifted his bandaged wrist.

"Yes." She motioned him over the threshold, into the parlor, her eyes taking on an unexpected sparkle. "You publish the new paper in town."

He swallowed hard. "Yes, ma'am. That's correct."

"Please, take a seat. I'll call Annis."

"Much obliged, ma'am." Hugh slunk into the room as Mrs. Jackson slipped gracefully from sight. Annis would be furious with him. He felt sure of that now. In fact, with every tick of the mantel clock, he knew this was the beginning of the end of everything good in his life. Annis. The newspaper. His relationship with Uncle Stickney. Even his friendship with Sid, should there be real feeling between him and Philippa.

Why did choosing to do right make so much come out wrong?

He slumped into an upholstered chair, indulging his self-pity until footsteps skittered across the hall. He looked up as a mountain of blue silk landed on the ground at his feet, the scent of roses rising to his nose. He held back a groan of desire as Annis rested her cheek against his knee.

"Hugh, darling! I'm so glad you're here."

CHAPTER 24

A TEAR SLIPPED down Annis's cheek as warm relief spread through her chest, into her belly. Hugh was here. Everything would be fine. But she'd expected to see joy in Hugh's expression. Instead the concern in his eyes felt like a blow to her stomach. Then she realized: He'd come to her home.

Uninvited.

Whatever had caused him to be so bold as to arrive at her front door couldn't be good. And after she confessed what else she'd done? He might run from her as fast and as far as possible.

She might have collapsed at the thought, except she was already on her knees beside him.

Hugh lifted her hand in his uninjured one, his mouth set in a grim line. Annis considered rising but feared her legs would refuse to hold her upright. Whatever he had to say, she must bear up under it, then be ready to make her confession.

"Annis—"

She flinched at the sternness of his tone.

"Annis." Hugh's voice took on its normal gentleness even as sadness covered him like a cloak. He forced his eyes to hers. "A new issue of the newspaper is being printed as we speak. An apology, of sorts."

Annis's spine snapped straight and rigid. Of all the possibilities running through her mind, that hadn't been one of them. "An apology?"

"Yes. For your editorial." His mouth crooked into a sorrowful half-grin. "Or rather that of J. A. Toledo, who everyone assumes to be me."

Heat flooded Annis's face, her breath locked inside her chest. She'd done it for them—for him—but that didn't seem to matter. He wasn't happy. And he'd come here to—

To what? To say he could never see her again?

Fine. If that was how he felt—

But maybe, maybe he'd give her another chance. She rested her forehead on his knee. "I'm so, so sorry. I never—I didn't—I—"

Thoughts and words refused to join hands, so she simply sat, hoping he could hear her apology in everything she left unsaid.

When she felt his hand rest on the top of her head, she fought for steady breaths, raised her head, but not her eyes. She couldn't bear to look at him. She didn't regret the words she'd written, as much as she regretted having put them in the paper without his knowledge.

"Annis?" He gently tipped her chin upward. "It was the prideful tone of the piece not your sentiments I disagreed with. Yes, the people of Toledo need to come together, not widen the gulf between them. But we will never sway them to that line of thinking by pretending we know everything. Words spoken in kindness are more effectual than venomous ones. And—"

"I know. I'm sorry. So very sorry." Annis wanted to reach out to him, to clutch his hand tightly in hers. But she refrained. Instead, her hands gripped one another. "Will you—can you— ever forgive me? I knew it was wrong to print the words without your knowledge. I was just . . . willful. I wanted—"

Hugh placed his hand atop hers. "I know what you wanted.

I want it, too. But not this way. Not anymore." He stood, held out a hand to Annis, to help her to her feet. "I'm here to speak with your father."

"You . . . what?"

"I want to speak with your father. No more hiding. No more lies. No more secrets. Not between us, or between us and those we love. Now, would you please——"

"Here we are." Ma swept into the parlor, a tea tray in her hands. "I thought you might be ready for some refreshment. Annis"—Ma turned and gave her a stern look—"would you please pour Mr. Hylton some tea?"

"Yes, ma'am." Her voice squeaked like a frightened mouse. She'd told Ma everything earlier. And Ma had told Pa. But what his reaction had been, she had no idea. Only that he left the house soon after. As to Hugh's plan . . .

Ma sat in her usual chair while a stunned Hugh sat in Pa's. Annis wondered if she were in the middle of a fantastic dream.

She extended a full cup to Hugh, her hand shaking free a drop that scalded her skin. She hissed at the pain. Evidently not a dream. Hugh was, indeed, sitting in the parlor, sipping tea and conversing with Ma, who hadn't batted an accusatory eye at either of them. She only hoped Pa would act in the same manner.

"My husband will be home shortly, Mr. Hylton. He had a . . . family matter to attend to. I suggest you stay to supper. Would that suit you?"

"Yes, ma'am. I'd be honored."

"Now, tell me how you and Annis came to be . . . you and Annis."

Annis sat quietly on the sofa opposite this strange tableau and listened to Hugh recount their relationship—without an implication of her role in the secrecy scheme—all the way until the moment when he and Ma met without introduction.

Ma cut her eyes toward Annis before setting her attention on

Hugh again. "And my daughter? What was her role in all of this?"

Annis bowed her head. Why was Ma going to make him say it when she already knew?

"She—well, she—" Hugh's stammer stabbed Annis's heart.

"They know." Annis spoke softly, but loud enough to be sure he heard. Her jaw tightened at the consternation in Hugh's gaze. "I told her everything. And she—she told Pa." Annis swallowed hard.

Ma gave Hugh a sorrowful smile before pinning Annis with her eyes. "I'm sorry I put you on the spot, Mr. Hylton, but I appreciate you seeking to protect Annis. My firstborn can be a handful. I hope you know what you are getting yourself into."

Hugh fought a smile. "Yes, ma'am, I think I do. But I'd be obliged for all the advice you can give me."

Ma's eyebrows jumped toward the ceiling, and a smile bloomed across her face. "I think you'll do, Mr. Hylton. Indeed, I think you'll do."

CHAPTER 25

HUGH LIKED ANNIS'S MOTHER. But was that really surprising? He adored Annis, in spite of her faults, so how could he not enjoy the presence of the woman who had raised her?

After a few more minutes of tranquil conversation, Mrs. Jackson left them alone. Well, not completely alone. Philippa sat smirking in the corner of the parlor as Hugh and Annis peppered each another with endless words of apology and forgiveness. By the time the front door opened and Mr. Jackson appeared in the parlor, Hugh had almost forgotten the greater object of his errand.

He leapt to his feet, moisture fleeing from his mouth, a lump settling in his throat. His heart beating against his chest like a bird caught in a cage. All while Annis rushed to her father, pressed a kiss to his cheek. Then she stifled a small cry as another man stepped into the room, hat in hand.

Uncle Stickney.

Hugh plopped back into his seat. What was his uncle doing here?

Mr. Jackson cleared his throat. "I thought it was time for a meeting, though I had no idea all the invested parties would be present."

Hugh ran a finger under the rim of his cravat. Had the fire grown larger? Or was he standing too near? He looked around, but the stove remained at the opposite end of the room.

With wide eyes, Annis led her father to his chair while Mrs. Jackson greeted Hugh's uncle as if there had never been any ill feelings between the two families.

Hugh glanced at Annis's father. He glared as if Hugh were a snake in a henhouse.

Which, perhaps, he was.

Uncle Stickney wore a similar expression, though whether because of Hugh and Annis or being summoned by his sworn enemy, Hugh had no idea.

"Annis, stop chattering and introduce me to our . . . guest, who apparently didn't have the gumption to introduce himself when we met previously."

Hugh winced but knew he deserved the set-down. Would he be able to overcome his discourtesy?

"Yes, Pa," Annis answered, her voice more meek and compliant than Hugh ever imagined it could be.

Philippa snickered. Annis sent her a scathing glance as she took Hugh's arm and led him to her father.

"Pa, this is Hugh Hylton, my . . ."

Hugh cleared his throat and stuck out his good hand. "Intended. Or will be, with your permission. Sir." He chanced a quick glance at Uncle Stickney, expecting surprise. Even anger.

He saw neither. In fact, was that a twinkle he spied in his uncle's eye?

Mr. Jackson looked at Hugh's outstretched hand for what seemed like an eternity before meeting it with his own. "Annis, Philippa." He addressed his daughters but kept his gaze fixed on Hugh. "I'm sure your mother could use some help in the kitchen."

Annis and Philippa fled the room before their mother, who gave her husband a long look, followed by a gentle hand on his arm as she departed.

With the women gone, sweat beaded at Hugh's temple and at the back of his neck. He hadn't meant to come right out and declare himself that way. He'd meant to ease into it. Even if Annis had told her father the truth, he hadn't had long to become accustomed to the idea of giving his daughter in marriage to a stranger. Let alone a man related to his greatest enemy.

An enemy who he'd brought into his home.

Perhaps he and Annis had misjudged both men. Perhaps they were willing to mend their differences after all.

Mr. Jackson motioned him to sit. Hugh perched on the edge of the nearest chair. "Sir, I know this has come as quite a surprise, but—"

"Surprise? More than two weeks after her homecoming, my daughter explains that she wishes to marry the publisher of that —that—" He glanced at Uncle Stickney and made an effort to calm. "*Newspaper.* That you formed a passing acquaintance during her time in Buffalo and a better one on the boat when her chaperone was indisposed. Not quite the man of integrity I envisioned winning my daughter."

"I—I understand your hesitation, sir."

"Hesitation?" Mr. Jackson snorted. "*Opposition* might be more accurate."

Hugh nodded, noting his uncle's face scrunching into a scowl. Hugh needed to appease both men. But how?

Taking a deep breath, he plunged to the heart of the matter. "I take full responsibility for that. I should have come to you the moment I arrived in town and let you know the state of things. And you as well, Uncle. Sh—*we* just thought perhaps it would be best for me to get the newspaper up and running—and prof-itable—before I came courting. Officially."

Mr. Jackson's eyes narrowed. "So you thought it would be better to see my daughter behind my back?"

Hugh noticed his uncle's fists clench. Perhaps reconciliation wouldn't come as easily as Hugh had hoped, especially if his uncle decided to defend him in this matter. The thought ignited a good feeling, but not necessarily a right one.

"N-No, sir. I—" Hugh looked down at the floor, gathered his wits before looking up again. "I'm sorry, sir. I was wrong."

Uncle Stickney leapt to his feet. Hugh followed, resting his hand on his uncle's shoulder. "You know it is true, Uncle. Mr. Jackson has every right to chastise. As do you." Hugh let his chin drop to his chest, hoping—*praying*—that he could earn the trust of both men.

"Pa, you know this was all my fault." Annis stood stiffly in the doorway, her hands clutching one another at her waist. "I'm sorry, Pa. Truly I am. Don't blame Hugh. He was always trying to do the right thing."

Mr. Jackson crossed the room and stood before her, his posture softening. "Hush, child. But please explain why you didn't just tell us?"

Annis shrugged. "When I learned of Hugh's . . ." She glanced at Uncle Stickney and swallowed visibly. "His *relations*, while we were on the boat, I guess I feared you'd—I don't know —dismiss him without a chance. I thought to surprise you after Hugh had proven himself. After you learned to love him as I do." She glanced at Hugh, took a deep breath. With a groan, she laid her head on her father's shoulder.

"You thought I would use Ben Stickney as a measuring rod against a man I didn't yet know?"

Annis caught her bottom lip in her teeth and nodded again.

"Oh, Annis." Mr. Jackson just looked weary now. As if this were one more disappointment in a long, unending line. He returned to his chair, reached for his pipe sitting on the small table nearby. After tapping tobacco into the bowl, lighting it and indulging in a few puffs, he turned to Hugh again, as if suddenly remembering his presence.

"Though I certainly do not hold you blameless, Mr. Hylton, I fear I know my daughter too well to discount her persuasiveness." He shook his head, but there seemed to be a sparkle of pride in his eyes. "If you are to marry her, you need to be aware that she tends to get what she wants."

Hugh nodded, Mr. Jackson's levity lifting him to confidence. "I understand, sir. But this entire situation has brought me a new understanding of myself." He glanced at his uncle, then Annis. "Of the fact that I can't always judge rightly by my own intuitions. I have to rely on something more sure. Something like . . . God. I'm new to understanding that He is interested in the details of my life, but now that I know, I desire to do what pleases Him first. Not what seems right to myself. Or to Annis."

Hugh looked into Annis's eyes for a long moment. It wouldn't be easy, but their relationship would be better now that they could go forward with the same foundation of belief. He squared his shoulders and faced Mr. Jackson.

"Sir, I promise I won't let her talk me into a course of action I know is wrong. And I do know it was wrong to keep to ourselves, especially after we arrived in town. Please forgive me. I would like the chance to recover your good opinion."

"And I would like to give it, Mr. Hylton."

Hugh turned to Uncle Stickney. "And yours as well."

Uncle Stickney nodded in quick agreement.

"But I would like to ask you both to do something for me as well—" Hugh blurted "—though neither of you have any reason to offer such favor to me."

Mr. Jackson grumbled softly, but after a poke from Annis, he nodded.

Hugh took a deep breath, looked each man in the face. "I would ask you both to commit to treat one another with kindness, even while holding to your different views."

Silence covered the room. Hugh kept his attention fixed on

Annis, on the pride shining out from her eyes. No matter what these men answered, she and Hugh were in agreement. And in the end, that mattered most of all.

Mr. Jackson put down his pipe and stood, extending his hand to Uncle Stickney. "Forgive me, Benjamin. I have not been the kind of man I desire to be. I have accepted the kindness and forgiveness of Christ and then withheld the same from you."

Everyone looked to Uncle Stickney. With a hint of laughter behind his eyes, he met Mr. Jackson's outstretched hand. "I accept—and ask the same of you, Gerald."

Their hands remained clasped a few moments more, as if sealing their newfound truce. Then Mr. Jackson turned to Hugh.

"Mr. Hylton, it is indeed a pleasure to make your acquaintance. I look forward to getting to know you, even if we never agree on the correct jurisdiction for our land."

"Yes, sir. Thank you, sir." From the corner of his eye, Hugh spied Annis, her face beaming with joy.

Then Mrs. Jackson appeared, her hands on Annis's shoulders, a smile wreathed in joy. "Now that we have that settled, let's all come to the table. Mr. Hylton, I assume you'll escort Annis?"

Without waiting for his reply, Mrs. Jackson claimed Uncle Stickney's arm and led him from the room. Mr. Jackson followed.

Hugh approached Annis, his heart full of hope and joy and gratitude. With his good hand, he cupped her face, used his thumb to dry the moisture beneath her eyes.

"Will you be my wife, Annis, dear?"

Annis's eyes glowed. "*That* was never in doubt, darling. No matter what happens between Michigan and Ohio, between my father and your uncle, we will always be us." She curled her hand into the crook of his arm. "Of course, I might have to make one condition of my acceptance of your kind offer."

He cocked one eyebrow. "And what would that be?"

Annis grinned. "That someone paint a more professional-looking window for the newspaper."

Hugh laughed and pressed a kiss to Annis's lips. "I think that can be arranged."

"Annis!" Mr. Jackson called from the dining room. "We're waiting."

AUTHOR'S NOTE

Yes, dear reader, there was indeed a "war" between Ohio and Michigan in 1835 for the strip of land which included the new city of Toledo on the shores of Lake Erie. And it did include a small skirmish between those loyal to Ohio and the Michigan militia trying to stop Ohio-sanctioned elections in the area. Benjamin Franklin Stickney—a real person, with real sons named One and Two—did indeed switch sides in the conflict. And Two Stickney did stab a Michigander with a penknife, resulting in the one injury of the minor confrontations. Mostly "the war" was a political battle between the governor of Michigan territory and the governor of Ohio. The issue was resolved in 1836. Obviously, Toledo ended up under Ohio's jurisdiction, but Michigan got the entire Upper Peninsula as compensation.

I took the liberty of fictionalizing the Stickneys even while using some of the facts of their lives.

A few people need to be acknowledged for their role in the creation of this book:

- Thank you to my writing prayer team—your ever-faithful petitions on behalf of my work are felt and appreciated. Thank you for your love and encouragement!

- Thank you to my husband, Jeff, who continues to support my efforts and who reminds me often that I am called to this, even when it seems futile.
- Thank you to my kids—Elizabeth, Aaron, Bailei, Nathan, and Mckenna—each of whom are a blessing I don't deserve.
- Thank you to Sarah Thompson for another amazing cover.
- Thank you to Charlene Patterson, who always makes my stories richer and deeper. (And more grammatically sound!)
- Thank you to Rachelle Rea Cobb for her attention to detail in the final edits. I'm so glad the Lord kept your schedule open for me!
- Thank you to my faithful readers! I hope you enjoyed your time with Annis and Hugh.
- And most of all, thanks be to my God, who continues to teach me and grow me in faith and hope and perseverance through every project. I am humbled and amazed.

ABOUT THE AUTHOR

Anne Mateer enjoys bringing history to life through fiction. She is the author of four WWI era novels and the Coast-to-Coast Brides novella series. Anne was a 2013 Carol Award finalist, has judged numerous writing contests, and occasionally teaches an online writing class. Anne and her husband, Jeff, have been married over 30 years and are currently living an empty nest adventure in Austin, TX. They love touring historic homes, lingering in museums, and visiting their young adult children in Texas, Arkansas, and Louisiana.

To stay up-to-date on the latest book releases, sign up for Anne's newsletter here.

For more information:
www.annemateer.com
anne@annemateer.com

 facebook.com/AuthorAnneMateer

 twitter.com/AnneMateer

 instagram.com/AnneMateer

NO SMALL STORM: A COAST-TO-COAST BRIDES NOVELLA

September 1815

REMEMBRANCE WILKINS—MEM to her friends and family—shivered, feeling to her bones the coolness of stone walls which never warmed. Eyes adjusting to the cellar's dimness, she lifted the candle lantern higher, wishing its small flame would throw out a bit of heat, as well as a larger circle of light.

There. In one of the perpetually shadowed corners, she spied a stack of bushel baskets within reach. Setting the lantern on the smooth dirt floor, she carefully unloaded the cloth bag at her hip. Apples. Twenty-two of them. Rhode Island greenings which would remain crisp and fresh in the cellar until the whole crop could be sold for transport beyond the port of Providence, Rhode Island. Or they were chosen for pressing into cider.

"But at this rate, I won't have a crop to sell until November!" Mem huffed the words under her breath, even though there wasn't a soul near enough to hear had she shouted. That was the glory of the farm—and the problem. Independence, yes. But often loneliness, too, if she were honest.

Her sister, Charity, often suggested hiring assistance, but Mem resisted. She needed the daily tasks to keep her occupied. And while a man in the fields would have his use, she had little desire for the help or company of any of that sex, now that her father had gone.

She lifted the lantern, the flickering candle inside barely skimming back the dark as she made her way back to the steps and into the sparkling day. In the flood of daylight, one quick breath extinguished the flame inside the lantern's iron frame. She set it on the ground as an errant curl tickled the side of her face. She hadn't time to stop and secure the wisp that had slipped loose of the pins. With squared shoulders, she stalked between rows of apple trees, all planted by her grandfather fifty years earlier, when Rhode Island was a colony, not a state. When this was British land, not American.

Near the back of the orchard, she spied the ladder still leaning against the trunk of a tree, its top lost in the profusion of leaves. Mem looked down at the yards of fabric covering her legs, wishing she could wear trousers, as her father had, instead of battling skirts and petticoats in order to secure an apple for her bag. But some things couldn't be wished away; they had to be endured. With the bag over her shoulder, she twisted her skirt and secured it between her knees. Then she set her foot on the first rung.

A rustling noise stopped her ascent. Not the gentle chorus of a sweep of breeze over hundreds of leaves. More like—

There it was again. A shimmy and a shake from somewhere above her head. Mem tipped her chin skyward, ready to flap her apron at a bold bird seeking a taste of fruit.

But the intruder she spied was larger than any bird.

Much larger.

"What are you—?"

A golden-haired boy of perhaps ten dropped from the

branches and landed crouched on the ground. Mem stared at him for a long moment, neither of them moving. Then he sprang to his feet and dashed away. Jumping from the ladder, Mem darted after him, trying to keep her feet from getting tangled in her hem. A cackle from behind brought her to a halt. When it sounded again, she whipped around to find another boy, similar in size to the first, squatting in the grass beneath the same tree, apple in hand.

"Stop!" Her shout carried across the orchard as she ran toward the newest intruder. He stood slowly, as if he needn't fear she'd catch him before he could scamper out of reach. Then he sank his teeth into the firm flesh of one of her apples. Juice dripped down his chin, onto his shirt. He opened his mouth to take another bite just as Mem grasped his arm. With a saucy grin, he threw off her grip and darted off in the direction of his accomplice.

Within moments, Mem stood alone on the road just beyond her apple trees, hands on her hips, chest heaving, lips mashed into a tight line. She hadn't recognized the two urchins, but she'd remember their faces, keep a lookout for them. Although she doubted she had any chance of discovery since they weren't already known to her. The population of Providence had grown greatly in the past few years. And now that the war with Britain had drawn to a close, there were so many new faces in and out of port. Mem grunted as she straightened the bag that had twisted in her haste, making sure the opening hung just in front of her hip. Then she returned to her orchard and started into the treetops again, tucking her skirt between her legs and climbing the ladder.

Two apples. That was likely all the boys had pilfered. She hoped. She leaned against the top of the ladder with a sigh and twisted a greening until it broke free from the branch. After gently dropping it into her bag, Mem's fingers found the next ripe apple and repeated the process. It wasn't as if she couldn't afford to lose two apples. Not with the bumper crop that had sprouted this year. A crop Papa would have crowed over.

Her eyes burned with sudden tears. Tears of grief. Tears of gratitude. She missed Papa's presence, his quiet faith and booming laughter—the loss too recent to be considered without pain. But to have him bequeath her the farm, allow her to remain at home and work the land she loved? Mem's heart swelled thinking of the words Mr. Benson had read the day after Charity and Mem watched Papa returned to the earth.

To my daughter Remembrance Wilkins, I bequeath the family farm and orchard, the land and its prosperity, for her lifetime use, after which it will be divided among any surviving children issued from either Remembrance or her sister, Charity Wilkins Hyer.

A position of independence was not always afforded an unmarried daughter. But Papa had understood. Mem had trusted him to provide for her, and he hadn't betrayed that trust. Unlike another man she'd had the misfortune to know.

The bag at her side grew bulky as her fingers worked by rote and her mind wandered. Then she eased back down the ladder, retrieved the lantern, lit the candle with the flint she kept nearby, and hastened once again into the cellar. Transferring the apples to the bushel basket, Mem shivered, this time with the understanding that while Papa had given her the farm and the orchard, it was up to her to keep them profitable—not only for herself, but for her nieces after her. Get the crop harvested and sold. Receive the money that would see her through the winter and spring. All of which would only happen after the greenings had been plucked from branches. And as of yet, she had barely cleared one tree.

Back out in the light of day, Mem stared in the direction of the road, the path the little thieves had travelled. Annoyance gave way to wistful fantasy. A sudden vision of her own sons climbing among the treetops appeared in her mind, their laughter ringing across the acres of land passed down through the generations, sun-browned legs churning in a game of hide-

and-seek. A whole family working together, as she and her sister had with their parents.

Foolishness! Mem stalked back into the orchard, chiding herself for entertaining dreams never meant to be hers. A family required a man. A trustworthy one. And those, she had learned, did not grow on any nearby tree.

No, she'd manage alone. Or wait for her nieces to grow up a bit.

Mem secured the ladder against another tree, but from the corner of her eye spied a figure coming up the road. A top hat and wide-shouldered jacket above a pair of trousers. A male visitor. Every muscle in her body tightened, reminding her of that which never long left her mind: She was a woman alone. Vulnerable. In body and reputation. She glanced down at the lantern still in her hand, fingers tightening on the handle. If she swung it hard at a man's head, it might provide enough of a stun for her to escape. Perhaps.

Just as her imagination caught hold of the idea, the man lifted his arm and waved. Mem squinted to see the face now coming into view.

Graham Lott.

Relief.

And then annoyance.

"Miss Wilkins!" He hurried forward until he stood within an arm span of her, his hat set at a rakish angle, a prodigious amount of ruffles on the cravat beneath his chin. Though he sported the fashion of a dandy, he didn't quite have the youth required to complete the look. Unless she missed her guess, he had fifty years to his credit. Twenty beyond her own three decades of existence.

"Mr. Lott." Mem dipped with her head and knees as he bent quickly from the waist. Then she had no choice but to give him her attention.

Mr. Lott didn't speak. Not at first. Instead, he surveyed the sturdy trees spreading out around them before his gaze roamed behind her, to the old stone house. Only after taking stock of the property did his eyes meet hers.

"I came to see how you were getting on with the apples, as your dear father asked me to." His mouth slid into the self-satis-fied grin that turned her insides cold as ice before they steamed to a boil of fury.

"I'm managing well, sir. But thank you for thinking of me. Now if you'll pardon, I must see to my orchard while daylight remains." She gave him another quick curtsy, hoping he'd take the dismissal graciously, although he never had before. Sure enough, he followed her though the trees, finally capturing her arms and stilling her beneath the canopy of leaves.

"You're clearing the trees on your own?" He let go of her then, circled the nearest tree, *tsking* with every step.

Mem sighed, lifted one hand, and rubbed the back of her neck. "I worked beside Papa all my life and oversaw much of the business while he was ill." Not quite the same thing as picking the apples by herself, but she brushed aside that bit of truth. She would find a way to get the crop in and prove to Mr. Lott—and everyone else—she could manage alone.

"But Miss Wilkins—Remembrance—there is no need for you to be a solitary soldier. Not when I have offered to take care of everything for you. You need only to consent to be my wife." He took hold of her hand while speaking in the condescending tone she'd come to know so well in the past six months. A tone he'd never used with her when Papa was alive. In those days, he'd simply been Papa's friend. But once they had committed Papa to the ground and the fact of her inheritance had become known around town, Mr. Lott had come boldly in pursuit of her, seeming to assume Mem's affection as his due. Affection she didn't hold for him.

How could she? He'd never asked anything about her inte-rior life—her hopes and dreams and hurts and fears, what resided inside her head and heart. She hadn't hesitated to declare her disinterest in joining herself to him. But while he'd respected her enough to back away from public pursuit, he tended to materialize from the shadows the minute she found herself alone. Alone in town, at least. He hadn't sought her at the farm before. Not until today.

She gently slipped her hand free of his grasp and took a step backward, praying he would take the hint and leave. "Thank you, Mr. Lott, for your . . . concern, but I believe I have made myself clear in the past and will continue to assert that while I am honored at what you have offered, I am quite determined to remain as I am. I have everything under control."

No need for him to know she did not. She simply had to behave as if she did.

He stood silent for a long moment, then tipped his had and bid her good day. Her knees shook as he walked away, unsure what she would have done if he'd persisted. But she had to make him understand that she had no intention of giving up her independence. Not for him. Not for any man.

Papa may have believed stubbornness her besetting sin, but he was wrong. Her stubbornness would be her only salvation. For if the orchard did not succeed, she feared the consequences would be unbearable.

PURCHASE NO SMALL Storm by Anne Mateer

ALSO BY ANNE MATEER

Playing By Heart

A Home for My Heart

At Every Turn

Wings of a Dream

Coast-to-Coast Brides novella series:

No Small Storm

Time Will Tell

Contributor to:

21 Days of Joy: Stories that Celebrate Mom (A Fiction Lover's
Devotional)

Made in the USA
Lexington, KY
01 November 2018